THANK YOU!

Books by Matt Christopher

Sports Stories

THE LUCKY BASEBALL BAT
BASEBALL PALS
BASKETBALL SPARKPLUG
LITTLE LEFTY
TOUCHDOWN FOR TOMMY
BREAK FOR THE BASKET
BASEBALL FLYHAWK
CATCHER WITH A GLASS ARM
THE COUNTERFEIT TACKLE
MIRACLE AT THE PLATE
THE YEAR MOM WON THE
  PENNANT
THE BASKET COUNTS
CATCH THAT PASS!
SHORTSTOP FROM TOKYO
JACKRABBIT GOALIE
THE FOX STEALS HOME
JOHNNY LONG LEGS
LOOK WHO'S PLAYING FIRST
  BASE
TOUGH TO TACKLE
THE KID WHO ONLY HIT
  HOMERS
FACE-OFF
MYSTERY COACH
ICE MAGIC
NO ARM IN LEFT FIELD
JINX GLOVE
FRONT COURT HEX
THE TEAM THAT STOPPED
  MOVING
GLUE FINGERS

THE PIGEON WITH THE
  TENNIS ELBOW
THE SUBMARINE PITCH
POWER PLAY
FOOTBALL FUGITIVE
JOHNNY NO HIT
SOCCER HALFBACK
DIAMOND CHAMPS
DIRT BIKE RACER
THE DOG THAT CALLED THE
  SIGNALS
THE DOG THAT STOLE
  FOOTBALL PLAYS
DRAG-STRIP RACER
RUN, BILLY, RUN
TIGHT END
THE TWENTY-ONE MILE
  SWIM
WILD PITCH
DIRT BIKE RUNAWAY
THE GREAT QUARTERBACK
  SWITCH
THE SUPERCHARGED
  INFIELD

Animal Stories

DESPERATE SEARCH
STRANDED
EARTHQUAKE
DEVIL PONY

The Fox Steals Home

The Fox
Steals Home

by Matt Christopher

Illustrated by Larry Johnson

Little, Brown and Company
BOSTON   TORONTO   LONDON

Library of Congress Cataloging in Publication Data

Christopher, Matthew F.
  The fox steals home.

  SUMMARY: Already troubled by his parents' divorce,
Bobby Canfield is further distressed when he learns that
his father, who has coached him in running bases, intends
to move away.
  [1. Baseball—Fiction. 2. Divorce—Fiction]
I. Johnson, Larry, 1949–   II. Title.
PZ7.C458Fp   [Fic]   78–17526
  ISBN 0–316–13976–9
  ISBN 0–316–13986–6pb

HC: 10 9 8 7 6
PB: 10 9

MV

*Published simultaneously in Canada
by Little, Brown & Company (Canada) Limited*

PRINTED IN THE UNITED STATES OF AMERICA

To Ed and Naomi

The Fox
Steals Home

One

"*STEP BACK*, Bobby. Let's go for two."
A pause. "Bobby! Wake up!"

The voice woke Bobby Canfield from his thoughts, and he looked at Coach Mark Tarbell, the tall, thin man standing near the right-side corner of the Sunbirds' dugout.

Bobby stepped back to the grass behind third base, suddenly conscious of the Cowbirds' batter that had just come to the plate. A kid in a uniform too large for him, with one pantleg hanging lower than the other.

Bobby's face colored slightly. He should have made that move without being told, but he had not been quite himself lately. It had been hard to concentrate on baseball

3

with all the trouble that had gone on back home.

He glanced over his shoulder at the scoreboard, and saw that it was still one out and the top of the third inning. So far both teams had nothing but goose eggs showing in the black squares.

"Pitch it to 'im, B. J.!" yelled Andy Sanders at first base. "He's nobody!"

"Lay it in there, B. J.!" Bobby chimed in, spitting into the pocket of his glove.

Try as he might, he couldn't shake off the thoughts that kept plaguing him. His mother and father's divorce papers had been filed only a few days ago, and it was like a bad dream. Every once in a while he felt almost convinced that he would wake up from it, but he had reached the point now where he knew it was no dream. It was all real.

"Come on, Bobby!" yelled second baseman Eddie Boyce. "Look alive there!"

Look alive? How could he when he felt so lousy?

He took notice that there were runners

on first and second, and vaguely remembered the sizzling grounder and the scratch hit that had got them on.

"Ball!" boomed the ump as B. J. breezed in a pitch.

"Don't walk him, B. J.!" pleaded Billy Trollop from center field.

B. J. laid his next pitch across the inside corner.

"Steerike!" announced the ump.

The Sunbirds exploded with approval. The fans with theirs. It was a hot June day, ideal for the shirt-sleeve crowd. Ideal for everyone except Bobby, to whom these last few days had all seemed the same. Terrible.

"Strike two!" said the ump as the batter swung at another pitch and missed.

Sherm Simmons tossed the ball back to B. J., who stepped off the mound and rubbed the ball a bit before getting back on the rubber again.

Checking the base runners, and then quickly shifting his attention to the batter, B. J. chucked in his next pitch.

5

Crack! It was a low bouncing grounder to Bobby's left side! Sprinting after it, he caught it in his outstretched glove, and snapped it to second base. Eddie Boyce was there, made the catch, and whipped it to first.

A double play! Three outs.

The fans applauded, and the Sunbirds praised Bobby for the play. He blushed slightly as he ran into the dugout and laid his glove on its roof. He liked the sound of that applause. It was the kind of music he could listen to anytime.

He wished he would hear another voice, too. That not-too-loud, mildly excited voice of his father's.

A couple of times during the game he had glanced at the crowd, hoping to spot the yellow cap that was his father's trademark. He hadn't seen it, and a sadness had crept into his heart. He wondered if his father would ever come to see him play again.

"Hey, Bobby! You're up, you old glove man, you!" grinned Eddie, picking up a bat

out of the upright rack. Eddie was second batter in the lineup. Bobby was first.

Bobby selected his bat, a yellow one with a taped handle. He put on his helmet and stepped to the plate. This was about the time he would usually hear that familiar voice of his father's ringing out, a cheerful sound that was most encouraging, especially when he needed it.

How much he wished he could hear it now.

He looked at Walter Wilson, the Cowbirds' big right-handed pitcher. After two innings of acute observation, Bobby figured him to be somewhat arrogant.

He let the first pitch go by. It was in there for a strike.

The first time at bat he had flied out to center. This time he hoped to even things up a bit. It would be awful to get up tomorrow morning knowing that he had played his first game of the season and hadn't gotten a single hit.

Walter stretched, jerked out his left foot,

came around with the ball, and winged it. It was in there, letter-high and straight as a string.

Bobby swung. *Crack!* He met the ball on the fat part of his bat and saw the white blur streak over second for a clean hit. A good, triumphant feeling went through him as he dropped his bat and sprinted to first.

He glanced at Walter, and saw the Cowbirds' pitcher picking up a handful of dirt. Rising up, the big boy tossed it disgustedly back to the ground.

I guess that hit got to him, thought Bobby, a hint of a smile on his lips.

He looked at the third-base coach, and couldn't believe what he saw — thumb to cap, to belt, to chest, and back to cap. The steal sign was on!

He sucked in his breath. What a surprise! He had never stolen a base before!

Well, he loved running the bases. He was fast. He had always outrun Billy Trollop in a sprint.

He waited for Walter Wilson to step into

the pitcher's box, then took a four-step lead. He stood, crouched — and sped back safely as Walter whipped the ball to first.

The first baseman tossed the ball back to Walter. Again Walter got on the mound, checked Bobby carefully, then delivered.

Bobby took off, losing his helmet halfway down the base path as he ran as fast as he ever had. Just as he neared the bag he saw the Cowbirds' second baseman reach for the ball, catch it, and bring it down for the tag.

But, in his anxiety to tag Bobby, the second baseman moved too quickly. Never having had complete control of the ball, he dropped it.

"Safe!" yelled the base umpire.

An enthusiastic cheer exploded from the Sunbirds' fans as Bobby rose slowly to his feet and brushed off his pants.

His father would have liked that. Yes, sireee.

After retrieving his helmet Bobby again

glanced at the third-base coach. This time it was finger to cap, to chest, back to cap, and then to belt. The bunt signal was on.

Eddie went after the first pitch. His position for bunting was perfect, but his execution of it wasn't. The ball popped up to the third baseman, who then zipped it to second before Bobby could tag up. It was a quick, surprising double play that left Bobby bewildered.

For the second time he rose with dirt-smeared pants. As he ran across the diamond to the front of the dugout before brushing himself off, he didn't fail to notice the smug look on Walter Wilson's round, sweaty face.

"Way to go, Walt!" yelled the Cowbirds' third baseman. "Let's take the next one! He's no sticker!"

Billy Trollop, the Sunbirds' third batter, made the player eat his words on the first pitch as he walloped it between right and center fields for a double. Andy Sanders repeated the feat, driving his two-bagger down along the left field foul line, scoring Billy. As if that weren't enough to prick Walter Wilson's ego, Snoop Myers belted a single over short that scored Andy.

That called for a consultation with Walter around the mound. It involved all four infielders and the catcher, each of whom presumably suggested to him how to handle the situation.

It probably did some good, for the next batter, Toody Goldstein, drew a walk. Then Hank Spencer flied out, ending the four-hit, two-run inning.

The teams exchanged sides, the Sunbirds standing somewhat more erect and looking self-assured now that they were enjoying a 2–0 lead.

Bobby, however, wasn't very happy about getting picked off at second base. He thought that if he'd had his wits about him he would have waited to see where the ball was going.

He could just picture his dad looking at him after that dumb play and saying, "No use being sore about it. It's over. Just try not to let it happen again."

He knew it wasn't his father's disposition that had been the cause of his parents' breakup. Nobody in this wide world had a more pleasant disposition than did his father. And it wasn't drink, the way it had been with Mr. Blake who lived down the block. Oh, Bobby's father had a glass now and then, but never enough to intoxicate him. He just didn't care for the stuff that much. As a matter of fact, neither did Bobby's mother. It was other things that had caused the lousy breakup. Their interests. Their priorities.

"Watch for the bunt, Bobby," cautioned Coach Tarbell.

The thoughts dispersed as Bobby glanced at the batter, a kid with hair the color of washed carrots. He bent his knees, let his arms dangle loosely at his sides, and suddenly imagined he was Pete Rose, Graig

13

Nettles, and Buddy Bell all rolled into one. He was sure that nothing was going to get past him. He was a staunch wall, able to stop anything that came his way.

B. J. pitched. *Crack!* A smashing line drive directly to the shortstop.

One out.

Well — what difference did it make where the ball was hit? As long as it was caught.

The next batter popped up to first.

"You're in the groove, B. J.!" Bobby yelled.

The Cowbirds' third batter came up, a small kid with blond curls sticking out from underneath his helmet. He let two pitches sail by him, one a ball, the other a strike. Then he laid into the third pitch as if he really meant it. The *smack!* of bat connecting with ball was solid. So was the hit, a sharp single over Bobby's head. Not even with a ten-foot ladder would he have been able to nab that one.

He stepped back, forgetting the famous triple personalities all rolled into one that he had imagined himself to be. Right now he was just Bobby Canfield, the not-so-famous third baseman for the not-so-famous Sunbirds.

Two

*B*J. *WALKED* the next batter, and a hopeful hum started among the Cowbirds' fans. They cheered as their next hitter stepped to the plate, a look of anxiety on his round face. He was chubby, and his helmet sat high on his head, leaving the ear-protective section almost too high to do any good. He held his black bat about four inches from the end of the handle, and waved it like a club.

Boom! B. J.'s first pitch went skyrocketing to deep right center, scoring both runners. Chubby, not blessed with lightning speed, had to be satisfied with a double.

It was all tied up now, 2–2. The Cowbirds were making a gallant comeback with two outs.

"Let's get back in the groove, B. J.!" yelled Bobby, spitting into his glove as he crouched in his spot at third.

"Take yer time, B. J.!" advised Snoop. "Take yer old time, boy!"

B. J. didn't have to be told to take his time. He had been doing that. He had seen lots of games on television in which the pitcher dilly-dallied on the mound, dug and redug the dirt around the rubber, wiped the sweat off his face, hitched up his pants and then studied the catcher's signs for five minutes before going about his business of pitching the ball. B. J. was already a vet in that department.

The kid in the uniform that looked two sizes too large for him, with the uneven pantlegs, came up. Bobby remembered the smashing grounder he had driven down to Snoop that Snoop had muffed. This kid was no slouch with the bat.

"Not too good to him, B. J.," said Bobby quietly.

B. J. checked the runner on second — more out of habit than because he expected the chubby guy to steal third — and delivered the pitch. It was high and inside.

His next pitch was almost in the same spot. His third was low for ball three.

Nervously, he began digging at the mound with the toe of his shoe, wiping the sweat off his face and hitching up his pants again. Then he studied Sherm Simmons's sign, which Sherm displayed with the professional aptitude of a Johnny Bench. Nodding agreeably, B. J. got into position and pitched.

It was down the middle for a called strike.

He tried to repeat the pitch, and grooved it, but this time Baggy Pants laid into it for a long triple to deep center field. The drive gave Chubby plenty of time to make it home for the Cowbirds' third run.

Somehow Bobby wasn't surprised about

the hit. Baggy Pants might not have cared how he looked in his baseball uniform, but as a player he was one hundred percent.

Two pitches later, a fly ball that must have climbed as high as the Empire State Building, almost disappearing out of sight, came down and was misjudged by center fielder Billy Trollop. The hitter got two bases on the hit, and credit for an RBI as the fourth run scored.

The fifth run came on a grass-scorching single between third and short. The third out finally came on a strikeout, which drew the loudest applause since the game had started.

B. J. walked off the mound with his head bowed. Until he reached the dugout he was a lone kid. Nobody said as much as a word to him.

When he sat down, Coach Tarbell offered him a few words of baseball wisdom. "Chin up, B. J. They just had a hot inning. No reason why we can't come back and do the same thing. Okay, Sherm," he said, turning to the catcher, who was stripping off his leg guards. "Let's start it off."

The back of his shirt sweat stained, Sherm walked to the plate and did just that, pulling a base on balls. B. J., not the best hitting pitcher in Lyncook County, bunted him down to second. The third baseman, who fielded the bunt, threw B. J. out at first.

Bobby got up from his kneeling position in the on-deck circle and strode to the plate, carrying his bat like Reggie Jackson. He looked eyeball-to-eyeball at the pitcher like Reggie Jackson, and swung like Reggie Jackson. But he missed twice.

Then Walter threw him a slider. The ball looked like the head of a snake coming around a tree. It headed for the plate, and Bobby swung again.

Crack! The ball sizzled out to short. The shortstop made the play to first, and Bobby was out. Sherm advanced to third.

Bobby made the turn to the right and trotted back to the dugout, completely forgetting that he was Reggie Jackson. Maybe he ought to try being Graig Nettles the next time.

Eddie slam-banged a double, scoring Sherm, and kept alive the Sunbirds' hopes of overtaking the Cowbirds. But Billy Trollop got up and pricked the balloon with a pop-up to third.

Cowbirds, 5–3.

Bobby looked across at Walter coming off the mound. The pitcher was squinting over his shoulder at the scoreboard in center field. Then he turned and looked grimly ahead. He was probably pondering a way to keep that lead, thought Bobby.

B. J. laid the first batter to rest with a strikeout. The next batter popped a high, towering fly over third base. Bobby got under it, feeling nervous all of a sudden as the ball started to play tricks on its way down. But he held out his glove, and he had it. Two outs. Then as he waited for the third batter to step to the plate, his mind began to wander.

You must try to see it from my point of view, too, Bobby. I'm your mother and I love you. You're my only child, the only good thing I have left. You must realize that your father and I just can't keep on living together like this. We'd be hypocrites to continue living together just because some people think that it's the proper thing to do. Well, it isn't, Bobby sweetheart. It's not the proper thing to do at all. Why, you can see for yourself how insufferable your father and I are getting to be toward each other. We're not happy and you're not happy. And it'll just be getting worse and worse, Bobby sweetheart.

The words were a fuzzy sound in the far recesses of his mind. There were tears in her eyes when she had spoken them, tears that had brought an ache to his throat.

The third batter lashed a furious drive past B. J.'s legs that sizzled out to center field for a single. And Bobby broke his daydream and began to fret. Another run would mean that the Sunbirds would need four runs to knock off the Cowbirds. And in this game the Sunbirds didn't seem to have that many left in them.

"Take 'im yourself, B. J.!" shouted Bobby. The next batter grounded out.

"Amen," murmured Bobby as he relaxed and trotted off the field.

"What inning is this, anyway?" B. J. asked as he plunked down on the dugout bench.

"Bottom of the fifth," said Coach Tarbell. "Andy! Snoop! Come on, you guys! Grab your bats! Start it off, Andy!"

Andy did — a corking single over first. Snoop bunted him down to second, sacrificing himself, although he made a gallant effort to turn the bunt into a hit.

Toody Goldstein, batting left-handed, looked sick on the first two pitches, missing both by inches. Then he connected with a fast pitch that drove Andy in for the Sunbirds' fourth run. Toody stayed on first, clapping proudly. It was his first hit of the season.

Hank Spencer stepped to the plate and began nudging his left shoe into the dirt as if he wanted to bury it. He took a called strike. Then Walter came back with another pitch that headed for the heart of the plate. It was a mistake. Hank laid into it, and the sound of bat meeting ball was music to the Sunbirds' ears.

It went for a home run.

On the mound, Walter's shoulders drooped as if something had happened to his collarbone.

"Send him to the showers!" yelled a Sunbirds devotee.

Sherm flied out to left, and B. J., who wasn't much with the stick, anyway, grounded out to short.

Sunbirds, 6–5.

In the top of the sixth, the Cowbirds connected with two hits, one walk, and two runs, to forge ahead, 7–6.

"Come on, Bobby!" encouraged Coach Tarbell as Bobby walked to the plate to start off the bottom of the sixth inning. "Let's get that run back — and more!"

Images of Graig Nettles, Pete Rose, and Buddy Bell floated through Bobby's mind as he strode to the plate.

Walter gazed at him through narrowed lids, stretched, and delivered. The pitch was wide. "Ball!" snapped the ump.

Bobby fouled off the next two.

Then Walter seemed to have lost sight of the plate, and Bobby walked.

Bobby trotted to first, then looked across the diamond at the third-base coach, who was watching Coach Tarbell standing at the side of the dugout. Whatever the sign was that Coach Tarbell related to the third-base coach Bobby didn't know. But the sign directed to him was clear as the hot shining sun.

Thumb to cap, to belt, to chest, back to cap. The steal sign was on.

Oh, man! Well, grease your joints and gas up your tank, Bobby. You're going to move!

Walter stepped on the mound, looked over his shoulder at Bobby, then started his delivery. Bobby took off, dirt puffing from his heels as he sprinted toward second base. Just before he reached it he saw the Cowbirds' second baseman covering the bag, waiting for the throw from his catcher.

Bobby hit the dirt, slid, and touched the bag a second before the Cowbird touched him with the ball.

"Safe!" called the ump.

On the mound Walter Wilson looked on, not liking the call one bit.

Three

*B*OBBY TRIED not to show it, but deep inside he was as proud as could be.

He wished again that his father was there, that his father could have seen him run. But, as before, the thought of his father reminded him of the divorce.

Why couldn't you two get along like millions of other married people? Why did it have to happen to us?

Bobby was nuts about baseball. But right now he was never happier to see a game coming to an end. It was a wonder that he had played as well as he had, because worrying about family problems had taken a lot out of him. And he hadn't been able to concentrate at the most crucial times.

"Drive 'im in, Eddie!" he heard Toody Goldstein yell. "Tie up the score!"

Who was to blame for the mess? His father or his mother? He didn't know. How could he? He didn't know every little thing that had gone on between them. No kid would. You didn't see everything. You couldn't hear everything.

Let's be careful about this, you and me. We don't want him to worry his little head over our problem. This is strictly between you and me, see?

That was the way the mess — the whole rotten mess — had seemed to exist to him. He didn't know when the smelly business had started. That was pretty difficult to tell. But it had been about a year ago when he had begun to see the signs: the cold tone of voice between his mother and father, the angry questions, the angry answers. Then the hours of awful silence, which were even worse.

29

Bobby shut out the ugly thoughts and concentrated on the batter, Eddie.

Eddie took three swings, striking out, and walked off the mound, his lips pursed.

Billy got up and popped up to third. Andy Sanders grounded out to second, leaving Bobby stranded.

Neither team scored in the seventh, and the game went to the Cowbirds, 7–6.

Eddie's parents came off the stands and hugged Eddie for the double he had hit. Andy's father came down and shook Andy's hand for the three hits he had pounded out. Hank's parents and his two sisters came down and hugged him for the single and the colossal home run he had smashed. Almost every one of the guys had somebody meeting him either to congratulate him on his hits, offer sympathy for losing, or both.

No one was there to meet Bobby. His mother wouldn't meet him of course. She didn't care sour apples for baseball. Or, he thought, for anything he did, for that matter.

"Hey, Bobby! Tough game to lose!" said a voice out of all that maze of voices.

Bobby looked around in surprise and saw that it was Mr. Trollop, Billy's father.

Bobby tried to smile. "That's right, Mr. Trollop," he said.

He walked home with some of the crowd, not saying anything to anyone, because no one said anything to him. He might as well be on the street alone.

"A broken home." That was a term he used to hear now and then at school, at play, and occasionally at home. It had meant very little to him. "Hey, Jimmy! Hear about Dave's parents? They broke up!" The usual response was "That right? Tough." Or, sometimes more frankly, "Oh? So what else is new?"

But, since the terrible thing had happened right in his own home, a "broken home" had suddenly taken on a definite meaning. For a long, long time there were the three of them — his mother, his father, and himself. And then one day he woke up and there were just the two of them — he and his mother.

It was too hard to believe.

There was a court trial about something to do with custody, a trial that had made him wish that he had never been born. Not that there was any violence between his mother and father. No, it was nothing like that.

It was just the strained calmness that had gone on between his parents, his mother's lawyer, and the judge. His father had not wanted a lawyer to represent him. He had said that he knew beforehand who would take custody of Bobby, and he was entirely agreeable to it.

It was that darned agreeableness that had bothered Bobby so much, because sometimes he felt that he loved his father more than he did his mother, even though he knew that the right thing to do was to share his love equally between them. That was hard to do sometimes, because both of them were so different. They had different interests. She liked partying, cards, bazaars, things that his father didn't care a hoot about. He was an outdoorsman. Give him a gun, or a fish pole, and a free weekend in the mountains, and you wouldn't find a happier man.

How the two of them had ever gotten together and married was beyond Bobby's imagination. And having him, their only child, must have just complicated the unimaginable union.

He arrived home, and saw a car parked at the curb — a shiny white car with tinted glass, chrome trim, and a CB antenna sticking straight up from the middle of the trunk. It was a car he had never seen before. Only a person rolling in dough would sport such luxurious wheels.

Bobby paused in his tracks and looked at the house. It was an old, two-story building that his father had renovated from an old two-story shack. Somebody had said that it had first been constructed as the village post office. That was only thirty years after the signing of the Declaration of Independence.

Whose car is it? he wondered. *A salesman's? An insurance man's?* It could be any one of a dozen people who might want to see his mother.

Maybe it was her lawyer's, Mr. What's-his-name. Hugo Ferris. But why should he want to see her again? The case was over, wasn't it? Well, maybe he just wanted to drop by and see how she was doing. A short, gray-haired man in his sixties, he had that warm, sympathetic quality about him that Bobby's mother seemed to have needed.

Or it could be one of her bridge-playing friends. She had a lot of them. Maybe they were having a chitchat, "woman talk," as his mother called it. His mother usually got home from work at ten after five, so whoever it was visiting her couldn't have been here very long.

He walked onto the driveway, noticing his mother's banged-up Chevrolet in the garage, and walked past the house toward the lawn in back. A hundred feet beyond was the lake, a spacious body of water covered with gently rolling waves and an array of sailboats and motorboats.

A three-foot-wide dock extended out to a hoist in which an inboard-outboard motorboat sat like a setting hen. It used to be Roger Canfield's favorite mode of transportation to various fishing spots on the lake. Since he had left, the boat had not been touched, although Bobby knew how to run it almost as well as his father did. He just hadn't felt like taking it out, that was all.

He sat on the edge of the dock and watched other boaters and water-skiers skimming across the lake, having the time of their lives. He had waterskied a few times himself. Man, it was fun. But that was before the breakup. Maybe, when he felt like it again — when the turmoil and the pain of his parents' divorce were behind him — he could get Billy Trollop and some other guys and go waterskiing again.

35

After about ten minutes, he thought about going up to the house. He was hungry, and his mother was probably expecting him, anyway.

When he reached the side of the house and looked around to the front, he saw that the white car was gone.

Well, if it were Mr. Ferris, the lawyer, his mother would have enjoyed the visit. He was an old guy, smart as a whip, but with a subtle sense of humor that would help Bobby's mother forget her cares for a while.

On the other hand, if it were somebody like Mrs. Trundle — that gossipy woman who used to be a neighbor and had moved to another part of town — Bobby's mother might have welcomed an earlier appearance by him.

Well, he didn't like to bother her when she was having company, that was all.

He entered the house through a side door, closing the door quietly behind him.

"Is that you, Bobby?" his mother's soprano voice carried to him from upstairs.

"Yes, Mom. It's me," he said.

"I'll be right down, dear," she said.

He went to the living room and started up the stairs to his room. He was only half-way up when she emerged from her room, wearing a bright yellow dress and high-heeled shoes, and carrying a small white purse.

"Bobby sweetheart!" she cried. "You look terrible!"

She stopped on the steps and brushed back his hair.

"You better get that uniform off and take a shower," she went on hastily. "And use a lot of soap."

"Where you going?" he asked her. He didn't remember her telling him that she was going somewhere this evening.

"Where am I going?" She stared at him as if that were the number-one dumb question of the day. "It's my bridge night, dear. I told you that this morning. Didn't I?" she added, a frown suddenly forming on her forehead. "Oh, I'm sorry, dear. Maybe I didn't. Anyway, it's Tuesday night, and you should know by now that I have a bridge party every Tuesday."

He looked at her pensively, wondering if she would tell him who her visitor had been.

But she didn't. She was too much in a hurry to leave. She just told him to get washed up, put on clean clothes, and to find his dinner in the oven.

"What is it?" he asked. He hoped it wasn't beans and corn again. He was getting tired of beans and corn.

"Spanish rice," she said, smiling.

He smiled back. Spanish rice he liked.

Four

*H*IS MOTHER woke him up the next
morning at 7:15.

"Gee, Mom," he cried, looking sleepily
at his Mickey Mouse alarm clock. His father
had bought it for him when he was eight,
and it was still ticking along as merrily as
ever. "It's the middle of the night!"

"You know what time it is," she replied,
her voice coming up the stairway in one
giant leap. "Get your b-o-d-y down here, so
you can wash up and eat breakfast. You've
got only fifteen more minutes before I have
to leave."

"Why can't you leave without me?" he

retorted. "I can make my own breakfast. All I eat is cereal, anyway."

"This morning I want you to have eggs," she said. "Protein is good for you. Now come down here and don't argue with me."

"O—kay," he said.

He shoved off the covers, rolled out of bed, and silently dropped upon the floor. The hardness of it was unbearable. But he lay there awhile, his eyes closed, until his back began to ache. Then he got up.

The sun was shining brightly through the curtains of his window, proving that it and the clock were both working against him. He dug clean socks and underwear out of his dresser, put them on, then put on his pants, shirt, and shoes, and went downstairs. He managed to do it without falling, which was somewhat remarkable since he had kept his eyes closed all the way down.

"Well, good morning, bright eyes," said his mother, who was already dressed in her work clothes and ready to go. She was a secretary in an office, and her work clothes were a trim-fitting dress and high heels. The rest of her outfit — a white, goatskin jacket that Bobby's father had bought for her two Christmases ago — was lying over the back of a chair.

" 'Morning," said Bobby, heading for the bathroom.

"Scrambled or sunny side up?" shouted his mother while he was washing his face.

"Sunny up!" he replied, finding it an effort to raise his voice enough to get it through the door.

After a while he managed to get dried and out of the bathroom. His sunny-side-up eggs, atop a piece of dark toast, were waiting for him, along with extra toast and a glass of milk.

"I want you to go to Grandma's today," said his mother as she pulled on her white jacket. "You don't have a baseball game again today, do you?"

"No," he said, sitting down on the chair

in front of the eggs. "Our next game is Thursday. Why do I have to go to Grandma's?"

"I want you to, that's why."

"When do you want me to go?"

"Sometime this morning. At least before lunch, so you'll have something else besides peanut butter and jelly for a change."

Grandma Reenie makes good peanut butter and jelly sandwiches, too, he almost told her.

"Good-bye, dear," his mother said, kissing him on the forehead. "See you this afternoon."

"'Bye, Mom," he said, and watched her go out of the door.

While he ate he heard the old Chev grinding away in the garage as his mother tried to start it. It suddenly sparked to life, then roared madly as his mother pressed down on the accelerator. *That's right, Ma,* he thought, smiling to himself. *Goose it. Clean out the carbon good, and maybe burn up the rings one of these days. Can't you remember Dad warning you about that?*

He finished his breakfast and put the dishes into the sink. Then he stared at them a while, pondering whether to wash them or not. One part of his brain told him he didn't have to, the other part advised him that he should.

He got to thinking about his mother struggling all day in front of a typewriter, typing up a pile of letters for her boss till her fingers were sore. And he grinned. *Oh, sure,* he thought. *I know that mother of mine better than anybody else does. She would never type so much to ever get her fingers sore.*

Nevertheless, the other part of his brain won. He did the dishes.

When he was finished he went into the living room and headed for the AM-FM stereo set. He'd put on an old Paul McCartney record, he thought, and then get the baseball scores.

His attention was drawn to the ashtray

on the coffee table. He had forgotten about his mother's visitor, but apparently whoever it was smoked, too, just as his mother did. He stared at the stubs of two cigarettes, one that he recognized as his mother's brand, the other, which was different. It had a tan band around the tip of it.

Suddenly he was Sherlock Holmes investigating the clue of the tan-banded cigarette stub. *Come on, Watson. Let's take a closer look and see what's elementary about it. Shall we, old boy?*

He stepped closer to the coffee table, and made a unique discovery. Both stubs had lipstick stains on them. Well, at least it wasn't a man. That would leave out the lawyer, Mr. Ferris. But that was as far as his investigative powers were able to go. He had determined that his mother's visitor was a woman: that was all.

For Mom's sake, he thought, *I just wish it wasn't Mrs. Trundle. That old bag of wind would talk the ears off of anyone who would listen to her. And Mom would listen to her even though she would never take Mrs. Trundle seriously.*

Glancing at the clock, he saw that it was nine-thirty. News time, followed by the baseball scores, would be coming on shortly. He didn't care about the news, but he had to listen to the scores. Music and sports. Without them you could throw your radio out the window.

At twenty-five minutes of ten he turned on the radio, heard the last bit about a railroad train derailment somewhere in Illinois, then the all-important, team-by-team scores in both the American and National leagues. The Yanks topped Boston. The Orioles downed the Brewers. The Oakland A's just eked out a victory over the California Angels.

He kept staring at the brightly lighted dial, looking at it as if hypnotized, while he listened to the rundown of the scores.

"The Mets three, the Cardinals two. Los

Angeles eight, the San Diego Padres one." The voice droned on, clear, monotonous.

His thoughts drifted to yesterday's game, and he saw himself hitting the old apple, getting on base, and sliding into second.

Man, he enjoyed running the bases, and making that steal. There was something especially challenging about it. Hey, Joe Morgan! Lou Brock! Watch out! There's a new base stealer on the way up!

"The Reds took it on the chin, five to four, from the Houston Astros, after winning four straight—"

"Oh, no!" Bobby cried, slamming his fists against the air.

After a while it was over, and he shut the set off. He took a quart bottle of orange juice out of the refrigerator, poured himself a glass, and drank it. Returning the bottle to the refrigerator, he wiped his mouth with his shirtsleeve and picked up his baseball cap. Blue, long brimmed, it was a symbol of his life's career.

He left the house, making sure that all the

doors were locked and that the key to the side door was placed on the lamp beside it.

Grandma Reenie and Grandpa Alex Morris lived on German Creek Road. To get to it you had to go up the road for a mile or so, then turn off to the left for about another half mile. It was a long, tiresome walk. By the time Bobby arrived he wished he had never started.

"You oughta have a bike," suggested Grandpa Alex, peering at Bobby through his trifocals. Balding, and gray around the edges of his hair, he still stood up straight as a pole and walked with the graceful bearing of a soldier.

"Mom thinks there's too much traffic where we are for me to have a bike," said Bobby.

"Pooshwah! It's a wonder she didn't worry about you walking up here."

"Are you hungry, dear?" Grandma Reenie asked him. Faint lines webbed the corners of her hazel eyes.

"No thanks, Grandma," he said.

"I've been meaning to telephone you, Bobby," said Grandpa. "But your grandmother keeps pestering me with one foolish job after another. How did your team make out yesterday?"

"We lost," said Bobby. "Seven to six."

"Lost?" Grandpa said it as if the word had a terrible taste to it. "How did you do? Get any hits?"

"One," replied Bobby. "And one walk. I also stole a base."

"You did?" A wide grin splashed over the old man's face. "Good! You're pretty good with the stick, are you?"

"Fair."

"Fair? That's not enough, boy. You've got to be good at something, get what I mean? If not with the stick, then with catching the ball. Otherwise you won't be worth more than a lick. What would you like to be good at?"

"Stealing bases," said Bobby.

48

"Stealing bases?" Grandpa's jaws dropped a few notches. "Why? You a whiz on bases?"

"No. I just like to run."

"Oh. So you just like to run. Well, I suppose it's the runners that score, isn't it?" He grinned warmly.

"That's right," said Bobby.

Five

I'VE GOT A theory about life, Bobby,"
Grandpa said, focusing his eyes through
the upper third of his glasses at his grand-
son. "And that is it's best to specialize in one
thing, at least. Two or three things are
better, but could be more difficult. So, *at
least* one thing. Get what I mean?"

Bobby nodded. Anyway, he *thought* he
got what his grandfather meant.

"What I'm saying is that if you want to
be a base stealer, go all out at it. Be good
at it. Be the best. Look how long Ty Cobb
held the base-stealing record. Then Maury
Wills comes along and breaks it. Then some-

body else comes along and breaks his. Why? Because they made a specialty of it, that's why. Get what I mean?"

Again Bobby nodded. He had known that his grandfather enjoyed baseball, but he had never dreamed that the old man was so psyched up about it. It was as if he wished he were young again himself to show Bobby what he was talking about.

"Practice is the key, Bobby," Grandpa Alex went on, emphasizing the word *key* to let it sink in. "Like everything else, a guy has to practice at his craft to be the best. Why work at anything if that isn't your aim? Get what I mean?"

Bobby grinned. "I get it, Grandpa," he said. He hadn't thought about being the best in anything. But, the way Grandpa put it, it didn't sound bad at all.

"Okay. Tell you what we'll do," said his grandfather. "I'll fetch my gloves and a ball, and we'll go to the ball park. We'll stop at your house first for you to put on your base-ball pants. Okay?"

51

Bobby nodded.

"Okay. Come on. We can put in about a half hour's practice, then come back and rest up before lunch." He turned and looked at Grandma Reenie sitting on the porch, crocheting an afghan. "Did you get all this chatter, Grandma?" he asked her. "Bobby and I are going down to the ball park. I'm going to make this kid into the best base stealer in Lyncook County."

"Just as long as you don't teach him to steal anything else," Grandma Reenie said, glancing up through her glasses but not missing a stitch. "And be back by lunchtime. I'm making chicken and dumplings."

"Half an hour. That's all we'll be gone," said Grandpa Alex.

He went into the house and stayed so long that Bobby began to wonder if he were ever going to find the gloves and bat. But he came out eventually, carrying them. They looked at least a hundred years old. *Well,* figured Bobby, *if they worked then, they should work now.*

They got into Grandpa Alex's green sedan and drove to Bobby's house, where he put on his baseball pants. Then they drove to the ball park that was about a mile toward the village, next to the school.

A few kids were knocking out flies with a softball in the outfield, but the infield was clear.

Bobby noticed his grandfather glancing toward the road now and then, as if he were expecting someone. But he thought no more about it as Grandpa Alex began issuing orders.

"Okay. Let's get down at first base. The first thing you'll need to learn is how to take your lead. It all depends on the pitcher, of course. That's the cheese you have to keep your eye on every minute. And if he's a lefty, you've got to be that much more alert. Get what I mean?"

They walked to first base. "Okay," said Grandpa Alex. "You're the runner, I'm the first baseman. Say there's a right-hander pitching. Okay. Take your lead."

Grandpa Alex stood in front of the first-base bag with one of his gloves, a bald-headed, skinny Dwight Evans. "Okay. He's looking over his shoulder at you. Now he's looking at the batter. He's throwing. Go!"

Bobby took off, slipped, almost fell.

"Come back, come back," ordered Grandpa Alex, not too kindly. "You stripped your gears, the worst thing you can do when you're stealing bases."

A car drove into the parking lot next to the first-base bleachers. Grandpa Alex saw it and flashed a knowing smile.

"Let's hold it a minute, Bobby," he said, watching the driver emerge from the car. "We've got some help."

Bobby sucked in his breath as he recognized the old blue car and the tall, middle-aged man wearing a yellow cap coming toward them across the field.

"Dad!" he said. An ache came to his throat.

"That's why you were so long in the house, Grandpa! You were telephoning Dad!"

Grandpa Alex's smile broadened. "That's right, Bobby. I knew he worked nights, so I thought I'd have him come over and give us a hand. You don't mind that, do you?"

"No. But you know what could happen if Mom finds out, don't you?" Bobby answered, fear taking the place of the warmth that had glowed in his eyes for that brief moment. "She can make him stop seeing me entirely."

"Pooshwah," snorted Grandpa Alex. "That's just a threat, that's all. Hi ya, Roger," he greeted his son-in-law with an outstretched hand. "Glad you could come."

"I wouldn't miss it for the world," said Roger Canfield. His brown eyes fastened warmly on his son. "Hi, Bobby. How you doing?"

They shook hands. "Good, Dad." Then his father wrapped his arms around the boy and held him for a minute. Bobby kept his eyes closed, giving his father squeeze for squeeze. *Oh, I love you, Dad!* he thought. *I really love you very much!*

They pulled apart, Bobby blinking his eyes slightly, then smiling at his no-holds-barred, cunning grandfather.

"Thanks, Grandpa," he said.

Even after the personal preliminaries were over, Bobby was still somewhat worried that his father was willing to risk their weekend get-togethers. But maybe his father figured it like Grandpa Alex did. Maybe he didn't think that Bobby's mother would carry out the threat, either, if she saw the two of them together now.

But how could she see them? She was cooped up in that air-conditioned office, typing up something for her boss. They were safe as money in the bank.

"So you want to be a base stealer, do you?" said his father. "And a darned good one, which is the only kind. Okay. Get on first base. Grandpa, how's your throwing arm? I know your eyes aren't the very best."

"Never was better," lied Grandpa Alex, who had played baseball until arthritis had incapacitated him at the age of forty-three.

"Okay. Get behind home plate and take that ball with you. You're going to try to throw Bobby out as he runs to second base."

"Eewowwwww!" yelled Grandpa Alex as he trotted like an old but nimble race horse to the position behind the plate. He was in baseball heaven.

Bobby, leading off the first-base bag, waited for his father to give the word. Suddenly it came. "Okay, Bobby! Go!"

Bobby took off as if he were catapulted. His father waited a moment, then yelled again, "Throw it, Alex!"

Grandpa Alex threw it. The ball got there a moment before Bobby did, except that it was about ten feet short. Bobby went into the bag standing up.

"Oops! Lost my target!" said Grandpa Alex.

"That isn't all you've lost," replied Roger, grinning. "But that's all right. The important thing is that it still is something for Bobby to run against. But next time slide, Bobby. Hit the dirt as if it's a close play.

You know how to slide, don't you? A little on your side and your knees a little bent. And come in hooking the base with your foot. You know all that?"

Bobby nodded. "I've done it before, Dad."

"Good. Okay, get on first. Try it again, and slide this time."

He tried it again, and Grandpa Alex tried to heave the ball farther, succeeding by about eleven inches. Bobby slid into the bag, hooking it with his right foot. All the major leaguers in the world couldn't have done better.

"Hey, kid!" exclaimed his father, his eyes glowing with pride. "You're a pro!"

Bobby grinned as he got up and brushed himself off.

"I want to get real good at it, Dad," he said.

They rested for a few minutes, then went at it again.

A car drew up slowly along the street, paused awhile, then accelerated and went on its way. The car didn't look familiar, nor did the man behind the wheel, but Bobby got worried, anyway. He still feared his mother's threat, even though his father and grandfather didn't seem to worry. She had meant every word she had said about his father's not being allowed to see Bobby at any time during the weekdays. Saturdays and Sundays yes, but not weekdays. It was in the papers that way, the papers that Mr. Ferris had filed away in his black satchel.

Six

*L*ET'S TRY something different," suggested Roger Canfield. "I'll get on the
mound and pitch. It might work out better
that way."

He strode to the mound, while Bobby
got into a runner's position on first base. His
father looked ten feet tall there, and like a
real pitcher as he stretched up his arms,
brought them down, then furtively glanced
over his shoulder at Bobby.

Bobby took a long lead, crouched, ready
to spring the instant his father made the
initial motion toward home.

Suddenly his father took his feet off the

rubber, twisted to the left, and made a quick throwing motion to first. Bobby raced back and stepped onto the bag, a wide grin spreading over his face.

"Would've had you," said his father. "That ball was right there in front of the bag."

"And if I was ump I would have called him safe!" boomed Grandpa Alex.

You knew where his heart lay.

Two kids came up and lay on the grass about ten feet from the foul line. They had long, straggly hair and wore moth-eaten, printed t-shirts. After glancing their way five or six times, Bobby finally made out what the printings were. One read I'M A MARTIAN, the other LOVE ME LOVE MY MONSTER.

Their presence began to irritate him, made him self-conscious. He thought that their watching him was preventing him from putting his best effort into his runs to second base. But his father offered no hint that he had slowed up.

Mr. Canfield had him running to third base, too, reminding him that there was no law against stealing the hot-corner sack if he could.

"Hey, man! You steal bases like a fox steals chickens!" one of the long-haired kids piped up.

"Yeah, you're some quick, sly fox," remarked the other.

A fox? Bobby conjured himself having a long snout and a long, flowing tail. He grinned. *Oh, sure, man!*

Another car slowed up on the street. Once again the premonition welled up in Bobby that the driver might recognize him and his father, squeal to his mother like a CIA spy, and drop the bomb that would separate him and his father. Again he didn't recognize the car, but the female driver looked familiar. Could she be one of his mother's bridge-playing friends? Or one of her bazaar friends? His mother was involved in so many things, she must have had a million acquaintances.

At last Grandpa Alex said that they had better call it quits, or Grandma Reenie would make him sleep with the chickens. They had gone way over the half-hour limit — by twenty-five minutes to be exact — and it was really high time they got back.

Bobby and his father shook hands again, reminding each other of their get-together Saturday morning at nine sharp, then started on their separate ways.

"Hey, Fox! Think you can steal a base like that in a game?" one of the kids yelled at Bobby as he started off the field with his father and grandfather.

"I'm going to try," he replied.

"I'd like to see you try it against Walt!" the other kid said. "Bet you'll never steal against him again!"

If I did it before, I'll do it again, thought Bobby. *Well, at least I'll try to do it again.*

As a matter of fact, he told himself, after the kind of workout he had just gone through with his father and grandfather, stealing against Walter Wilson should be as easy as ABC.

"See you at the next game, Fox!" the other kid promised.

Bobby smiled and waved. Fox, he thought. What a name they had tagged onto him. Crazy guys.

He and Grandpa Alex stopped at his house on their way to Grandpa's home. He changed back into his other clothes, then rode on up to his grandparents', wondering just how angry Grandma Reenie might be, because they had returned later than promised.

It would be something if she made Grandpa sleep with the chickens. The image of his grandfather snuggling down among all those hens and roosters made Bobby smile.

As it turned out, she never mentioned it, though she did appear slightly put out that they were nearly an hour late for lunch.

65

Bobby showered first, then his grandfather did, and it wasn't until he sat at the table that he realized how famished he was. He had two big helpings of chicken and dumplings, and then a triangle of strawberry pie, all of which filled every nook and cranny of his belly.

"You won't be able to eat tonight," Grandma Reenie said as she collected his empty plates.

"You wanna bet?" Grandpa Alex said, small eyes twinkling.

Bobby smiled. He felt like a stuffed sausage, and didn't think he'd be able to eat for a week. Anyway, his mother undoubtedly had someplace to go tonight and wouldn't have the time to make a big supper. Since the separation she kept herself so busy it seemed they never sat down to a big supper anymore.

It turned out that she didn't go out, and that she didn't make a big supper, either. Maybe it was because Bobby told her what he had eaten for lunch. "All that for lunch?"

she ranted. "What got into that crazy head of your grandmother's, anyway? She seldom cooks for lunch. In that case, it'll be canned stew tonight. I can stand a rest from cooking after slaving in that hot office all day. Whew!"

"Hot?" he said. "I thought it was air-conditioned."

"Not this week it hasn't been. The air-conditioning unit has been kaput and Lord knows when it'll be working again."

The woes of a working mother. Wonder if I'll work in a hot or an air-conditioned office when I get a job? Bobby asked himself. *Never. Not if I can become the best base stealer of the year and pull in a couple million bucks. Then retire when my legs give out, say at thirty.*

They played the Finches on Thursday under a boiling hot sun. For two and one-half innings it was a pitcher's battle, both hurlers managing to keep the batters hitting the ball into the mitt of a defensive player just as if it were planned that way. Ollie Hitchcock, the Sunbirds' right-handed pitcher, so self-conscious of his height that he walked slightly stoop-shouldered most of the time, seemed to become more erect each time he strode off the mound.

"Let's change those eyeballs to numbers," said Coach Tarbell, referring to the zeroes decorating the scoreboard. "What do you say, Ollie?"

Ollie seemed not to have heard him as he rummaged around the bat rack for his favorite home run slugger, found it, and walked to the plate. Ollie, who wore glasses and wanted to be a concert pianist when he grew up, slugged the first pitch to short for the first out.

Here we go again, thought Bobby as he left the on-deck circle and replaced Ollie's position in the batter's box. He tried to conceal his nervousness by pretending he was Graig Nettles, gripping his bat so hard that his knuckles shone white. Sixty feet away from him, standing like a gargantuan on the mound, stood Bung Sweeney, the Finches' ace right-hander.

Bung fired two pitches that the ump called strikes, getting well ahead of Bobby to be able to waste a couple.

But the next pitch was in there, too, and Bobby swung. *Crack!* The ball hopped like a rabbit through the hole between third and short, and Bobby was on.

Glancing at the third-base coach, he got the sign he was hoping for. The steal sign.

"Hey, Fox! Let's see what you can do now!" yelled a voice from the first-base bleachers.

Bobby didn't have to turn around to see whose voice that was. It belonged to one of the two long-haired kids who had watched him practice base stealing. He should have known they would be here today.

Bung got on the mound, stretched, looked over his shoulder. Bobby, leading off as far as he dared, waited for that right moment, that split second that could make the difference between success and failure.

Swiftly, Bung stepped off the rubber and whipped the ball to first. Bobby got back, hardly a fraction of a second in time.

"Watch it, Bobby," warned Snoop Myers, the first-base coach.

The first baseman tossed the ball back to Bung. Once again Bung got ready to hurl, and Bobby got ready to run. This time Bung fired his pitch in, and Bobby took off. Dirt sprayed from the heels of his shoes as he sprinted for his target, second base. He lost his cap and helmet as he slid into the bag, hooking it with his foot long before the second baseman tagged him with the ball.

"Yay! Thataboy, Fox!" yelled the long-haired kid, as other fans joined in with a chorus of cheers.

Bobby rose to his feet, brushed himself off, and looked toward the third-base coach, Hank Spencer. Hank was looking toward the bench, getting the sign from Coach Tarbell. In a moment his attention was back to Bobby. He went through some crazy signs that meant nothing, indicating that Bobby was to play it safe.

Eddie Boyce, batting, slammed a two-one pitch over second, and Bobby raced to third and then home as if a dozen bears were on his tail.

Billy Trollop grounded out, but Andy Sanders kept the spark alive by blasting a double to deep left. The Finches' left fielder rifled the ball in to third as Eddie touched the bag and headed for home.

"Hey, get back, you idiot!" Hank yelled at him. "Get back here!"

Seven

*T*HE THIRD baseman whipped the ball home just as Eddie slid on his posterior in a valiant effort to bring himself to a stop. Reversing direction, he half ran, half crawled back to the bag. With a last gallant effort he stretched out his hand and touched the bag a fraction of a second before the Finches' third-sacker caught the ball and tagged him.

"Safe!" roared the base umpire.

The third-sacker stared at the ump. "What?" he shouted, started to argue, then seemed to have second thoughts about it and turned away.

"You goon," said Hank to Eddie, who had risen to his feet and was brushing the dirt off his pants. "Didn't you see me signaling you to stop?"

"I thought you were signaling me to keep going," said Eddie.

"Oh, man," Hank moaned, striking his forehead with the flat of his hand. "I'm going to get you a pair of glasses."

Snoop Myers lashed a liner through second for a clean single, scoring both Eddie and Andy. Then Toody struck out.

Finches 0, Sunbirds 3.

"Hey, Fox, you did all right!" yelled one of the kids as Bobby sprang from the dugout and headed for his position at third.

"Thanks." Bobby grinned. He had at least two good supporters, that was for sure.

Someone sitting on the third-base side of the bleachers chuckled. "Nice steal, Bobby."

The sound of the familiar voice struck a sensitive chord, and Bobby glanced toward the bleachers. It was his father! He was sitting there in the fourth row, wearing that familiar yellow cap.

"Thanks, Dad," his heart answered.

He was thrilled and surprised to see his father there. It was something he had hoped for, but not really expected.

The Sunbirds kept the Finches from scoring, and it looked as if the Sunbirds would go through the inning scoreless, too, as Hank flied out and Sherm fanned. Ollie Hitchcock, whose ability as a hitter had not ever been a major threat to any opposing team, stepped up to the plate.

Bung got two strikes on him, and was on his way for his third strikeout as Ollie went into his third consecutive swing. But this time a resounding crack exploded as bat met ball, catapulting it through the hole between left and center fields. The unbelievable became believable as Ollie made it to second base standing up.

"Knock him in, Bobby!" encouraged a fan as Bobby strode to the plate.

He felt comfortable and confident, none

of that nervousness he had felt the first two times up. That 3–0 lead could do that for you.

Bung whistled two pitches by him, both balls, then wrangled in a strike. The fourth came in knee high and Bobby swung, meeting the ball squarely for a single over short. Ollie raced in to home, boosting the lead another notch.

Bobby looked for the steal sign, eager to give his legs another workout. He stood there, some five feet away from the first-base sack, leaning forward, both arms swinging loosely. Since he had decided to excel as a base thief, nothing was more important anymore. Nothing, that is, as far as baseball was concerned.

But he didn't get the steal sign. Apparently Coach Tarbell wanted him to play it safe.

Eddie stroked the first pitch to center field for the third out. Discouraged because he was deprived of his chance to attempt another steal, Bobby trotted to the bench, got his glove and headed to his position at third.

He took a quick glance at his father, who met his eyes and smiled.

The Finches, coming up for the top of the fifth inning, still could not find the handle of Ollie's pitches, and went back out to the field, a bunch of defeated sad sacks.

Again the Sunbirds picked up a run as Andy scored on a triple to deep left off the bat of Snoop Myers. The Finches, unable to find the magic that would give them any momentum at all, picked up only horse collars again in the sixth and seventh innings, and the Sunbirds walked off with the win, 5–0.

The first thing Bobby did was head for his father, who descended from the bleachers and met him near the first row.

"Three hits and a stolen base," said his father happily. "Congratulations. You're playing like an old pro."

The third hit had come in the sixth inning, giving Bobby three-for-four for the day. His mind easily tallied up the percentage: .750. If he continued hitting like that he'd be the envy of the league.

"It's my best game so far," said Bobby proudly. "But it's only my second," he added, smiling.

"Yeah. Well, you'll do all right in the rest of them, too," his father assured him. "You've got the spunk. That comes first. All the rest will follow."

A voice cut in. "Hey, Bobby! You coming?"

It was Billy Trollop, walking toward the gate with his parents and another couple.

"I've got to go, Dad," said Bobby, anxious to keep talking with his father, yet fearful that if his mother found out about it she would try to sever their relationship forever.

"Bobby, wait," said his father. "I've got something to tell you."

Bobby started away, his heart on a cloud for being able to see his father for just that brief moment.

"Tell me about it Saturday, Dad," he said.

"I've got to go now."

"But, Bobby, that's what I want to tell you about."

Bobby stopped, his heart suddenly pounding. He waited for his father to continue, afraid of what he was going to hear.

"I won't be picking you up on Saturday," said his father. "I promised to go fishing with some buddies of mine. We were in high school together, and we haven't seen each other in years. You understand, don't you?"

Bobby's heart stopped, and he felt riveted to the ground, unable to believe what he had just heard.

"But you know that Saturdays and Sundays are—" he started to say. He couldn't finish. The words choked in his throat.

Understand? Sure, I understand, Dad, he wanted to say. *You'd rather fish with your friends than be with me!*

Well, go ahead! Don't let me interfere with your fun. I'm just your son. You don't have to keep a lousy promise to your son.

Go ahead. Go fishing. Have a good time, Dad.

"Hey," said Billy, as Bobby stopped beside him. "You okay?"

"Yeah, sure. I'm okay."

I'm fine. Just fine.

I wish I were dead.

"Where are you going?" his mother asked him.

"I'm going to take the boat out for a while."

The instant he spoke he realized how bitter he sounded. But he didn't apologize. He didn't feel like apologizing to anybody this morning, not even to his mother.

"Well!" she said. "And a good morning to you, too. What's eating you? Would it have something to do with your father?"

He had the porch door open, letting in the cool, morning breeze that was blowing from the lake.

"That's right. He's not going to pick me

up this morning. He's going fishing with some of his buddies."

"He *what?*"

He started out the door.

"Bobby! Come back here!"

He stepped back into the house, closed the door, but didn't look at her. She had her hair up in curlers. Every Saturday morning she had her hair up in curlers, whether she was going anywhere that evening or not.

"What's this about him going fishing with his buddies?" she asked, her eyes focused on him like blue agates.

"He told me that."

"When did you see him?"

"Thursday. At the game."

"Is that so?" she said, suddenly ruffled. "Even after he agreed not to see you during the week."

"Well, I saw him there, and after the game I went over to talk to him a minute." Bobby felt that he should be truthful about it. "So you can't blame him for that."

She kept looking at him. "No, I suppose if that's the way it was, I can't blame him."

She was silent a while.

"Okay if I go now?" he asked, anxious to get out of there.

"I suppose so," she said stiffly. "Since it's what you want to do."

Eight

*H*E WENT DOWN to the beach and walked out on the narrow dock. Unlocking the large wheel at the side of the hoist, he gently lowered the boat into the water. It was a sixteen-foot, fiberglass Starcraft with a 110-horsepower engine that lay exposed in the stern. The cover for it was in the small beach house up on shore.

The boat was not in top-notch shape because, like a lot of other things he kept promising to do, Roger Canfield had kept promising he'd fix the gas line running from the tank under the forward deck to the carburetor, but never had taken the time to do it. The leak from the brass fitting had become a sore Bobby had become accustomed to, and since it had not caused any trouble so far he had practically forgotten about it.

He inserted the key into the ignition, started the engine and backed the boat out of the hoist. Some ten yards out, he shifted the throttle gently forward, and got the boat moving ahead. The lake was a little choppy, causing the craft to rock. Shoving the throttle harder forward forced the bow to raise up high and the boat to speed over the water, shooting sheets of spray on either side. In a moment the bow settled down to where it belonged.

He drove toward the middle of the lake, noticing other powerboats cutting a swath through the water, too; and sailboats whisking silently along, stitching their way through the crests and troughs, puffed-out sails holding the boats in that limbo space just short of keeling over. Bobby had never sailed before, but someday he would like to.

He turned to the left, and then to the right, weaving a crazy pattern of waves behind him. With the throttle wide open, the noise from the engine was so loud he wouldn't have been able to hear himself talk if he tried.

But he didn't care. He had to do something to get the thought of his father out of his head.

He turned the wheel sharply to the right, putting the boat into a ninety-degree angle, and almost panicked as he found himself heading directly into the path of an oncoming powerboat. That boat, too, was speeding at full throttle — or near it, judging by its sound.

Quickly Bobby spun the wheel to the left, as the other craft turned to the right. Even so, both crafts veered so close to each other that very little daylight shone between them. Bobby, feeling like a fool, couldn't blame the anger he saw on the other driver's face.

Oh, man, he thought. *I'd better head back for home before I ram this boat to kingdom come.*

He turned the wheel till the bow of the boat was aimed in the direction of home, then straightened it out.

The ride, instead of erasing the unpleasant thoughts of his father, had almost resulted in a disaster. He couldn't win.

He finally reached the hoist, cranked the boat up on it, and took the key into the house. His mother wondered why he was back from his ride so soon. "Just had enough of it," he said, bending the truth somewhat. No sense worrying her about what almost happened. She might never let him go out alone in the boat again.

He had barely hung the ignition key on a nail in the laundry room when he decided to keep on going through the front door for a walk to Meadow Park. There was usually some action going on there — a scrub ball game, tennis, something.

"Now where are you going?" his mother

asked as she looked at him from the dryer where she was removing a load of clothes.

"Out," he said.

"Out where? Do I have to squeeze every word out of you?"

"Meadow Park," he said.

"Okay. You're going to be back by lunchtime, I hope."

"I'll try," he said, his voice not any friendlier than hers.

He opened the door and went out.

I don't know, he thought. *I'm twelve and she keeps treating me as if I were still eight or nine. When will I ever be a grown-up to her?*

Meadow Park was about half a mile away. It was located on a piece of land jutting out into the lake, and contained a picnic area besides the playground for the kids. As Bobby had suspected, a baseball game was in progress — with a tennis ball instead of a baseball — and at first glance he recognized most of the kids who were playing.

Then his attention riveted on the tall

right-hander on the mound. Even though he wasn't wearing his monkey suit, he looked familiar. He was Walter Wilson, the Cowbirds' pitcher.

"Hey, there's Bobby Canfield!" yelled Nick Tully, another player for the Cowbirds. "Come on, Bobby! We're lacking a man!"

He hesitated, wondering whether to play or not. In a minute he consented. "Where do you want me?" he asked.

"On third," cried Nick. "Hey, Tommy! Get out to center field, will you?"

Tommy Elders, a regular for the Swifts, a team that the Sunbirds were scheduled to play next, ran out to center field, and Bobby took over at third. One thing about playing baseball with a tennis ball, you didn't need a glove.

He could hardly believe that he was playing on Walter Wilson's team. Walter Wilson, the Cowbird's crack pitcher.

A pop fly was hit to first, then a fast-hopping grounder was hit to Bobby. He did a Pete Rose fielding job with it, and heaved the ball to first. Unlike a Pete Rose throw, though, the ball took off like a rocket, sailing over the first baseman's head.

"Hey, man! What an arm!" yelled Toody Goldstein, covering right field.

"Moon's only five foot two, not ten foot eight!" exclaimed another Sunbird, Eddie Boyce.

Nothing like a bad throw to invite insults, thought Bobby. *Good thing it was just a scrub game.*

A towering fly ball to center ended the half inning. Bobby walked off the field, his mind still on the wild throw to first. Scrub game or not, such gross throws preyed on a guy's mind. Just because you tried to do your best in a real game, there was no reason in this wide world why you shouldn't try your best in a scrub game, too.

"Bobby!"

The voice came from someone near the lilac bushes flanking the road behind the ball park.

Bobby turned, and stared in surprise. It was his father!

"Dad!" he cried.

What was he doing here? He was supposed to be with his friends. Fishing.

His thoughts went topsy-turvy. The sight of his father twisted things all around for him.

His father motioned to him. Reluctantly, Bobby approached him.

"I stopped at the house," his father said. "Your mother told me you were coming here."

"I thought you went fishing," said Bobby.

"I called my friends," said his father. "I'm meeting them tonight, instead. Is that okay?"

Bobby's heart went up to his throat. "Sure is," he said.

"What do you want to do? Stay here and keep playing with the kids, or do something else? Anything."

Bobby thought a minute. "Can I practice base-stealing a bit?" he asked. "This would be a good time. The ball park's probably empty. I think that most of the guys are here. Then we could see the Giants play the Foxes. If you'd like to."

His father smiled. "Why not? Come on. We won't need a ball. Just your legs."

Bobby yelled to Nick. "Nick, I've got to go. Sorry! Thanks for letting me play."

"Okay!" Nick yelled back.

Bobby turned back to his father, saw him gazing attentively at one of the players.

"See somebody you know, Dad?" he asked.

"Well — yes. But never mind. Come on."

Instinctively, Bobby glanced over his shoulder, and met the strong, silent gaze of Walter Wilson. Was he the one at whom his father had stared?

But why him? How in this world could his father know Walter?

He pushed the thought to the back of his mind as he turned and followed his father to the car.

They drove to the ball park. Bobby had

guessed right; there was no one there. He practiced running the bases, getting the jump on the pitcher, and stealing second and third.

When he got tired, he rested and once suggested to his father, between breaths, that they ought to have a stopwatch.

"No way," replied his father. "You're not training to be a professional, or for the Olympics. This is just to teach you the right way to run and steal bases, and to develop those abilities as you keep playing. I don't want you to strain, either. Too much of this stuff at one time could injure a muscle, hurt you for life. We don't want to take a chance on doing that."

They had barely started practicing again — the last time today, his father promised, before they would head for the city park to see the ball game — when a car drove up slowly and parked at the curb behind the high wire fence. There was a woman in it: a stranger, at least to Bobby.

The horn honked. Bobby looked at his

father. "She honking for you, Dad?" he asked wonderingly.

His father, standing on the pitcher's mound, looked over his shoulder.

"Darn," he said, half under his breath. "What does she want?"

Nine

I'LL BE RIGHT back," he told Bobby, and walked briskly across the diamond to the car. He talked with the woman for a few minutes, then came back. The woman started up the car and took off.

"Okay," said his father, back on the mound. "Get on first. We'll go through it once more, then head for the game."

His attitude had changed. Bobby could tell by the sharp way he spoke, by the expression on his face. Had something the woman had said to him bothered him that much? Who was she, anyway?

But Bobby didn't ask his father who she

94

was. He didn't think it was his business to pry.

Finished with the base-stealing practice, Bobby brushed himself off as thoroughly as he could and got in the car with his father.

"You're probably wondering who that woman is," Roger Canfield said.

Surprised that his father should mention it, Bobby shrugged. "I don't care who she is," he said.

"She's a friend," explained his father, nevertheless. "A widow. Met her at a bowling party."

"That's okay, Dad. You don't have to tell me about her."

He didn't want to hear about her. The less he knew the better. He still had hopes of his mother and father's reuniting again sometime when the dust from their marriage problems had settled. Maybe that was looking for a miracle, but he hated to see another woman enter his father's life, making sure that the miracle would never happen.

They drove to Municipal Park and got

there a few minutes before the Giants–Foxes game started. They stayed the full nine innings, even though it was one of the dullest games Bobby had ever seen in his life: 1–0, in favor of the Foxes. And that single run by virtue of an error. Super super dull.

"Fast game, but Dullsville," said Bobby as they drove out of the parking lot.

"You should've said something," said his father. "We would have left earlier."

"I was just hoping for something to happen," said Bobby. "But nothing did."

His father laughed.

"Are you still going to church with your mother?" his father asked after a brief silence.

"Nine o'clock every Sunday," answered Bobby.

She was almost fanatic about it. She never missed.

"Good. You never know when you'll need someone to lean on, someone other than a mere human being. Know something? I just bought one of the best sellers ever published."

Bobby didn't know much about best-sellers, except for something like *Charlotte's Web* or *Fog Magic*, kids' books that his father had probably never heard of. Or books on famous athletes. He gulped them down like cereal.

"I don't know any best-sellers, Dad," he admitted.

"You know of this one," replied his father. "It's the Bible."

Bobby looked at him, a little embarrassed. "We've got one, but I've never read it. It's pretty long."

Roger Canfield shrugged. "I know, but I've been reading one chapter at a time, and I'm about a third done with the book already. Can you believe it? Me reading the Bible? I bet if your mother heard about it she'd flip."

His dad didn't press about the Bible reading, but Bobby could tell it meant something special to him.

They stopped at a red light. "There's a fair on in Meadville. Like to go there tomorrow?"

"I'd love it," said Bobby.

"Fine. I'll pick you up at the usual time, eleven o'clock."

Bobby had the sudden fear that their day had ended, that his father was going to take him home. But two blocks farther on, Roger Canfield turned right and pulled up in front of a diner.

"I'm starved, aren't you?" he said.

Bobby grinned. "Something like that," he admitted.

He enjoyed these little surprises that his father often pulled on him. They made their stay together so much more fun.

They went inside, found a vacant booth, and sat down. Roger Canfield took off his yellow cap, set it beside him on the seat, and surveyed his son. "It's been a great day, Bobby," he said happily.

"Sure has, Dad," replied Bobby. "Wish we could do it every day."

"Me too."

Idle talk. Wishful thinking. Even before his mother and father had split up, he and his father hadn't spent a heck of a lot of time together. But he was around, at least. And they often had indulged in their own private talk, which included sports, a topic his mother had placed at the bottom of her list of favorite subjects.

They ordered from a menu that a waitress brought them, and took their sweet old time putting the food away. When they were finished Roger Canfield left a tip for the waitress, paid the check, and followed Bobby out of the door.

"Feel better?" he asked.

"I'm stuffed," confessed Bobby.

His father drove up to the house at a minute of eleven on Sunday morning, picked up Bobby, and drove to Meadville, twelve miles away. The fair was already in full swing: the ferris wheel revolving slowly, every chair occupied; the stiff, plastic horses

of the merry-go-round jumping up and down in slow motion; rockets spinning in a wide circle; a fat man wearing a derby four sizes too small for him selling helium-filled balloons. On the midway, hucksters on makeshift stages were trying to inveigle the people into their tents to see "the famous chicken woman," "the alligator man," and "the two-headed goat."

"Interested in something like that?" Roger Canfield asked his son.

Bobby shrugged. "Oh, I don't know." He wasn't sure if he was or not.

"Come on," urged his father. "Most of this stuff is a lot of baloney to separate people from their money. But if you've never seen one of these shows before, now's the time."

They bought tickets to the "famous chicken woman" show, and saw a small, thin woman whose chest protruded like a chicken's and whose skin resembled a chicken's.

"I expected to see feathers," said Bobby.

"Maybe she's been plucked," his father chuckled.

The "alligator man's" somewhat brown, scaly skin was undoubtedly what had earned him his title. Bobby left the tent disappointed, although he hadn't known what to expect. An alligator man with a long snout and a snapping tail? *That's* an alligator, man!

"Had enough?" asked his father.

"Had enough," echoed Bobby.

They rode on the ferris wheel and the rocket, and tried winning prizes at the various concession stands. By evening, when they ended the day by eating a light dinner of hamburgers, salad, and ice cream, Bobby's prizes were an accumulation of sorts — a rag doll, a plastic cat, a bamboo cane, and a glass coin bank. The items were practically worthless, but they were souvenirs just the same of a day that he would remember for the rest of his life. Today was the day he had gone to the Meadville Fair with his father.

Roger Canfield drove him home, and hugged him tightly before Bobby got out of the car.

"Thanks, Dad," said Bobby, trying to keep a lump from rising to his throat. "I've had a real great time."

"So have I, Bobby," said his father. "See you next Saturday."

"Right."

When Bobby got to the door of the house he found it locked. He located the key on the lamp near the door casing, unlocked the door, and went in.

On the kitchen table was a note: *Dear, I won't be home till late. If you're hungry, there is tuna fish in the refrigerator. Make a sandwich. And there is cake in the cupboard. Love, Mother.*

Ten

ON TUESDAY the sun was playing hide-and-seek with the clouds, and a light breeze was teasing the trees when the Sunbirds met the Swifts on the Lyncook School Ball Park.

During infield practice, before play began, Bobby saw a left-hander warming up for the Swifts. He was Lefty Thorne, a kid with nothing but a straight ball and a slider. He didn't need anything else from what Bobby had heard through the grapevine.

"Hey, Fox! How many bases you going to steal today?"

The voice came from the third-base

bleachers. Bobby glanced there and saw the two long-haired kids. He wasn't surprised. They were his best fans.

"Got to get on base first," he said.

"Right!" the other agreed, grinning broadly.

In a few minutes the ump was shouting "Play ball!" and Bobby went up to the plate, his nerves jumping. He hated left-handed pitchers.

Lefty Thorne looked seven feet tall as he took his stretch, brought down his arms, then delivered. The ball seemed to come directly at Bobby, and he backed away from it.

"Strike!" said the ump.

Bobby looked at him, but the ump's attention was drawn to his counter, which he was holding in the palm of his left hand. It was, Bobby thought, a devious way of ignoring him.

Lefty rifled in another pitch for "Strike two!" and Bobby stepped out of the box. He took a deep breath, hoping that it would settle him down, and stepped back in again.

This time Lefty's pitch was outside, and so was the next. His fifth delivery came barreling in with something on it, because it started in toward Bobby, then headed out, like a snake that had seen something and wanted to get away from it.

Bobby swung. Bat met ball squarely and Bobby, dropping his bat, sped down the first-base line. The blow was a single over short, just six inches shy of being caught by Joe Morris, the Swifts' shortstop.

"There you are, Fox!" one of the kids yelled at him. "You're on!"

Bobby looked at third for a sign — any kind of sign — and got it. Play it safe, it said.

Eddie let the first pitch go by. It was a ball.

Bobby looked for the sign again. This time he got what he was hoping for — thumb to cap, to belt, to chest, and back to cap. The steal was on.

He waited for Lefty to get on the mound,

and took a lead. Remembering the pointers his father had given him, he made sure that his lead wasn't too big. Facing first base, a left-hander had a better advantage over the base runner than a right-hander did.

Lefty stretched, lowered his arms slowly, then quickly took his foot off the rubber and snapped the ball to first. Just as quickly Bobby shot back.

He was safe. But it was close.

The first baseman tossed the ball back to Lefty, and once again Bobby got ready. This time, as Lefty lowered his arms and started his pitch to the batter, Bobby was off like a shot.

He ran as hard as he could, but he felt as if his legs weren't really obeying his impulses. They didn't seem to be covering the ground as fast as he wanted them to.

He was within three feet of the bag when he saw the Swifts' second baseman reach for the ball and put it on him. By then he had slid in, a fraction of a second before the player had tagged him.

"Safe!" said the ump.

Bobby rose to his feet, not too happy about his run.

"Thataway to go, Fox!" yelled the two kids, almost in unison.

"Nice run, Fox!" another fan yelled.

Bobby winced. What had those crazy guys done? Tagged him with a nickname that might spread like measles?

With a one-and-one call on him, Eddie tied onto the next pitch and lofted it to center field, where it was easily put away for the first out.

Hank Spencer stepped to the plate and laid into the first pitch for a long foul strike. Coach Tarbell had shifted the lineup slightly, moving Hank up from seventh batter to third to take advantage of his long-ball hitting.

Lefty missed the plate on the next two pitches, then blazed one in that barely cut the inside corner. Two balls, two strikes.

Hank didn't appreciate the call. He stepped out of the box and looked out over the third-base bleachers for what might be a sign of sympathy from the fans. He got nothing but subtle chuckles and a sarcastic comment from a Swifts fan instead. "The plate's behind you, big shot."

Finding no sympathy, Hank returned to his position in the box and waited for Lefty's next pitch. It was a slider, and Hank laid into it. *Crack!* The ball shot out to left center for a clean hit. Bobby scored. By the time the ball was in, Hank was sliding into third.

"Hey, Fox!" exclaimed Andy Sanders, batting next. "You going for a base-stealing record or something?"

Bobby shrugged. "Something," he said, grinning. "Like runs."

He didn't mind the praise coming at him from the bench and the fans. It made him feel good, even though he wasn't thoroughly satisfied with himself. Well, at least, he had beaten the ball to the bag. That was the idea for a steal.

Andy Sanders grounded out, bringing up

Billy Trollop. Billy fouled a pitch to the backstop screen, then belted a line drive through second, scoring Hank. Snoop Myers couldn't find the handle of Lefty Thorne's pitches and went down swinging.

Sunbirds 2, Swifts 0.

B. J. Hendricks had it easy going with the Swifts' first two batters — a groundout to short, and a pop-up to Bobby.

Dick Flanders, the Swifts' left-handed left fielder, tied onto one for a sharp drive to center, only to get a single out of it. Then center fielder Tommy Elders poled an Empire Stater to Billy out in deep center, and that was it for the Swifts.

Jake Shakespeare, a utility outfielder, led off for the Sunbirds in the top of the second, and flied out to right. Neither Sherm nor B. J. was able to do any better, and the Swifts were back up to bat.

Butch Rollins, their burly catcher who sweated even when he wasn't doing anything, tagged B. J.'s first pitch for a two-bagger. Another double and a single followed, tying up the score.

Nuts, thought Bobby. *There goes our lead.*

A gangling redhead smashed a hot grounder down to third, snapping Bobby out of his doldrums. He scooped it up and whipped it underhand to second. Eddie caught it and snapped it to first. A fast double play.

Bobby pounded a fist proudly into the pocket of his glove. A play like that gave you a lift every time.

Lefty Thorne, socking a high bouncer back to B. J., ran only partway down to first as the Sunbirds' hurler caught the ball and tossed him out.

Bobby, leading off in the top of the third, waited out Lefty's pitches and earned a base on balls. Right off, Toody Goldstein, coaching at third, gave him the steal sign.

Taking a good lead, Bobby got set. He waited for Lefty to pass that limbo position, that point in his act when Bobby was sure that Lefty was going to throw either to first, or to home.

Standing on the mound like a tall mannequin with his arms and head moving in slow motion, Lefty glanced over his shoulder at Bobby. Then he looked back at the batter, quickly raised his leg, and started his delivery. Bobby took off.

About six feet from second base, as he saw the baseman nab the ball thrown to him by the catcher, Bobby slid. The baseman tagged him on the foot.

"You're out!" yelled the ump.

Bobby stared up at him, his heart pounding. But the man in blue had his face and forefinger pointed in another direction.

"Too bad, Fox!" one of the long-haired kids remarked as Bobby ran off the field.

"Can't win 'em all!" added the other.

More sympathetic remarks came from the guys on the bench. But sympathy wasn't what he needed, nor looked for. There was something he was not doing right. Perhaps he could have taken a bigger lead. Another foot might have made a difference. You can't be a Joe Morgan if you don't get the jump on the pitcher.

Bobby felt worse when Eddie tagged a pitch through an infield hole for a single. If he had been safe at second, he could have scored.

Hank poled a long fly to center that looked as if it were going over the fence. Instead, Tommy Elders, the Swifts' center fielder, got back in time, leaped and made a one-handed stabbing catch.

Then Andy started the ball rolling with a triple, followed by a walk by Billy, and a single by Snoop Myers. When the merry-go-round was over the Sunbirds had garnered two runs and were back in the lead.

Sunbirds 4, Swifts 2.

In the bottom of the third, B. J. held the Swifts down to a single and no runs. In the fourth, Sherm's single and B. J.'s walk looked as if another scoring inning were in the works. But Bobby flied out, Eddie grounded out, and Hank went down for his first strikeout.

The score was still unchanged as Bobby stepped to the plate in the top of the sixth. There was one out, B. J.'s pop-up to first.

Lefty breezed in a straight ball that was too good to be true. Bobby laid into it, smashing it hard down to third. Dropping his bat, he bolted for first, while out on the hot corner Steve Malloy missed the handle of the fast hop and let the ball streak through his legs.

Steve let his feelings go public by taking off his glove and throwing it against the ground, puffing up a cloud of dust.

As for Bobby, he'd take first base regardless of how he got it. Glancing toward third, he saw the steal sign coming at him again. Thanks, Snoop, he wanted to say. That's what I'm looking for.

This time he took a slightly extra lead and, as Lefty began his delivery, he took off.

He was there with time to spare.

"Hey, Fox! You did it, man!" someone shouted. It was one of his long-haired fans.

Eddie, a strike on him, let another pitch go by. "Ball!" cried the ump.

Bobby glanced at Snoop, and couldn't believe his eyes. Snoop was giving him the steal sign again! What? With one out? What was Coach Tarbell thinking of?

Well, so what? Stealing bases was his cup of tea. His *business*.

He took a long lead, got back quickly when Lefty tried to pick him off.

He resumed his position when Lefty got back on the mound, then took off like an Olympics hopeful as Lefty delivered.

Eddie let the pitch go by. The catcher caught it, whipped it hard to third, and the third baseman put it on Bobby.

"Out!" yelled the ump, loud enough for every person in the stands to hear him.

Bobby was sick. Rising gloomily to his feet, he trotted back to the dugout.

"Chin up," said the coach as Bobby

plunked himself down on the bench near him. "I wanted to see if you could do it. I figured, too, that if you got on third, an infield hit — no matter if it went through or not — would score you."

"Sorry it didn't work," said Bobby disappointedly.

"That's okay. Forget it."

Eddie flied out, ending the half inning.

The Swifts weren't able to bunch enough hits together during their next two trips to the plate, so lost to the Sunbirds 4–2.

After the hoopla was over — the Sunbirds praising the victory to each other — and the teams began to leave the field, Bobby heard his name called, and his heart soared to his throat. He'd recognize that voice anywhere.

"Dad!" he exclaimed as he saw his father coming toward him.

Someone was with him. A woman. She looked familiar.

Suddenly Bobby recalled where he had seen her before. It was at the ball park. She was the one who had driven up in a car, the one his father had gone to talk to.

There was a third person directly behind her.

Walter Wilson.

Eleven

*B*OBBY, *THIS* is Mrs. Wilson," said his father. "Mrs. Norma Wilson. And I guess you know Walter."

"Yes, I know him."

Bobby's eyes shifted to Walter, who was in his baseball uniform, and then to Mrs. Wilson. Embarrassment flushed his cheeks. Crazy thoughts rattled like rocks in his head. He didn't need it in writing to see that his father had found himself another woman. And that she was Walter's mother.

She put out her hand. He took it, reluctantly.

"Hello, Bobby. I'm glad to meet you. Your father has told me so much about you.

Walter must bring you over to our house sometime. We can have lunch together. Or even dinner. Would you like that?"

He shrugged. "I suppose so."

She had a slight build and brown hair, and wasn't bad-looking, much as he hated to admit it. Walter, whose hair and eyes resembled hers, seemed like a giant beside her.

Her fingers relaxed; their handshake, thank goodness, was over.

"We just got here," explained his father. "Saw the last half of the inning. Congratulations."

So he didn't see me running the bases, Bobby thought. *He didn't see me getting out sliding into third.*

"How did you guys make out?" he asked Walter in an attempt at conversation.

"We won."

"Who did you play?"

"The Swallows."

It was like dragging the answers out of him.

"How many hits did you get?" Walter suddenly asked him.

The question came as a surprise, and Bobby found himself staring at Walter.

"Two," he said.

"Pretty good."

Walter seemed tense, and met Bobby's eyes for only a moment at a time. *He's nervous*, thought Bobby. *Maybe he's going through the same kind of strain that I am, because we're living under similar conditions. Both of us have only a mother living with us.*

But I see my father once in a while. Walter never gets to see his. His father's dead.

"We better go," said Bobby's father. "See you again, Bobby."

"I must hurry home to make supper," murmured Mrs. Wilson, smiling jovially. "It was so nice to meet you, Bobby. And don't forget my invitation, will you?"

"No, I won't, Mrs. Wilson. It was nice meeting you, too."

He watched them leave. *That Walter,*

Bobby reflected. The kid certainly would never be known as a big talker.

He looked for Billy Trollop, found him, and rode home with him and his family.

After supper that night the doorbell rang. Bobby went to answer it. A woman stood there, a tall, pretty woman in a pink blouse and white slacks. She was carrying a cardboard box.

"Hello. I'm Mrs. Thorne," she said pleasantly. "Is your mother in?"

Almost automatically his eyes were drawn to the car at the curb. A white Charger.

A wisp of a smile curved his lips. So she was the one whom the car belonged to.

"Yes," he said, and, turning, called to his mother. "Mom! Someone here to see you!"

"Be right there!" replied his mother from another part of the house.

Bobby invited the woman in, and closed the door behind her. She wasn't smoking, but she could be carrying a pack of cigarettes in that huge white purse of hers. He took notice of her mouth, too. It was generously covered with lipstick, the same color that he had seen on one of the cigarette butts in the living room ashtray.

There was a hurried shuffling of sandals on the stairs, an overture announcing his mother's arrival. "Oh, hi, Jane," said Joyce Canfield, loose strands of hair dangling along the sides of her face. "You must forgive me. I'm cleaning, can you believe it? Seven-thirty in the evening, when most people are watching television, playing cards, or swimming in their pools, I'm cleaning!"

Mrs. Thorne smiled. "The woes of keeping house," she said.

"You said it!" said Bobby's mother, brushing back her hair. Her eyes fell upon the box Mrs. Thorne was carrying. "You have my order? So soon?"

"The cosmetics have already been manufactured, Joyce dear," said Mrs. Thorne sweetly. "All the company had to do was pack it and ship it."

"Fun-ny," replied Bobby's mother. She suddenly seemed to remember that Bobby was there, and officially introduced him. Bobby and Mrs. Thorne shook hands.

"He's a handsome boy, Joyce. And about the age of my own son. How old are you, Bobby?"

"Twelve."

"My David's thirteen. You should know him. He pitches for the Swifts."

"Oh! You mean Lefty? Sure, I know Lefty. Everybody does. We beat his team today."

"Don't I know it," she said. "He's been moping around the house ever since he came home from the game."

Bobby's mother invited her into the living room where they sat down, lit up cigarettes, and chatted. That's what they had been doing the day he had come home and found the cigarette butts in the ashtray, he thought.

He excused himself, went to the den, and turned on the TV, just in time to watch a final chase scene on his favorite detective show. The hero captured his man, subtly accepted the accolades from his superior, and the case was closed.

It was shortly after lunch the next day when someone rang the doorbell. Bobby answered it. It was Billy Trollop.

"Hi, Billy," he greeted, somewhat surprised. It wasn't often that Billy came over to see him anymore. "What's new?"

Billy's visits used to be as regular as clockwork, but ever since the divorce of Bobby's parents they had dropped to almost nil. Bobby supposed that Billy was embarrassed to come anymore. But he wasn't sure and he didn't ask.

"There's a guy down on your beach wants to see you," said Billy.

"Who?"

"Walter Wilson."

"Walter Wilson?" Bobby's eyebrows arched. "What does he want?"

He had no idea where Walter lived, except that the burly pitcher for the Cowbirds didn't live in *this* neck of the woods.

"I think he'd like a ride in your boat," said Billy.

"What?" Bobby frowned. *Walter walked all the way here for a ride in my boat?* he thought.

He remembered yesterday's meeting with Walter and his mother. That brief meeting showed him that Walter was in the same boat that he was. Maybe Walter was in one that was even worse. He didn't have a father, and that must have hurt him. But, being a tough kid he didn't want anyone to know how he really felt. Maybe he needed someone to talk it over with.

I think I know how he feels, Bobby thought. *Since my parents have divorced I have felt awfully alone. Why is it? Is it that because when we're hurt we're afraid to open up and maybe be hurt more?*

"Well, what shall I tell him?" asked Billy.

"I'll talk with him," said Bobby.

They walked down to the beach, and Bobby saw Walter standing on the dock by the hoist, looking at the interior of the boat.

"Hi, Walter," greeted Bobby.

"Hi," said Walter. "How are you doing?"

"Okay."

"I came over to take a ride in your boat," said Walter. He held Bobby's eyes for a few seconds, then bent over, picked up a flat stone and launched it out over the lake. The stone hit the water, skipped half a dozen times, then disappeared.

"I don't know whether I should," Bobby said.

Walter peered at him. "Why not? Your father said it's all right. That's why I came. He said that you wouldn't mind taking me out for a ride."

Bobby looked at him. "My father said that?"

"Of course. Look, do you think I'd walk all the way over here if he hadn't asked me to? He said to phone you first, but I didn't think it was necessary. I figured that you'd

127

be somewhere around here, anyway." He launched another stone across the surface of the lake and watched it skip. "I walked about two miles to get here. You want me to walk back without a ride?"

Bobby thought a minute. "Wait here," he said finally. "I'll get the key."

Twelve

*B*OBBY GOT the key from the house and returned to the dock. He released the catch that secured the iron wheel, then lowered the boat into the water.

"Okay. Get in," he said to Walter.

Walter got in.

"Don't you want to come along?" Bobby called to Billy.

"No, thanks," said Billy.

Bobby shrugged and inserted the key into the ignition, started the engine, and backed the boat slowly out into deeper water. Then he turned the wheel and cautioned Walter, who was crouched against the gunwale behind him, to hang on. Then he thrust the throttle forward. The boat lurched ahead, bow rising, engine roaring. After a few moments the bow settled down, and the boat bounced over the choppy water.

A sailboat was in his path, tacking toward the east shore of the lake, and Bobby turned the wheel slightly to avoid running into it. As he headed toward the north end of the lake, he began to wonder why Walter really had come over. Maybe he wanted to talk about their parents. Bobby didn't know if he wanted to do that. He hardly knew Walter well enough to judge his sincerity.

He glanced over his shoulder to see what Walter was doing, and almost jumped out of his skin as he saw the boy trying to light up a cigarette.

"No smoking, Walt!" he shouted.

At that same instant the blazing match that Walter was holding to the tip of his cigarette went out. Ignoring Bobby's warning, he tore another match from the book, and struck it. Again it went out.

This time he knelt down. And, with the protection of the windshield, he started to strike another match.

Mounting anger, mixed with an equal proportion of fear, surged through Bobby. "Walt! Did you hear me? No smoking, I said!"

As the second warning left his lips, he saw Walter flick the cigarette over his shoulder. His intention was for it to go overboard. It didn't. The wind took it and swept it back into the boat, into the engine compartment, where it seemed to die out for a moment, but blazed back to life.

"Get that cigarette!" Bobby started to yell. But just then the red tip of the cigarette touched the leaky gas line and ignited it.

The explosion that followed was loud, shattering, bomblike. Bobby saw the blinding flash of fire, then was knocked against the instrument panel and the wheel. Dazed and scared half to death, he turned and saw Walter lying on the deck, flung there by the explosion.

Remembering that the gas tank was underneath the forward deck, his fear increased a hundredfold. Rushing to Walter and grabbing him by the shoulders, he yelled shrilly, "Get up and jump out! Quick, before the gas tank explodes, too!"

They jumped out, and began swimming as fast as they could away from the boat. A moment later the gas tank did exactly what Bobby had said it would. It exploded, blowing a gaping hole through the bow, and sending flames billowing madly into the air. Rocked by the terrific blast, the boat heaved. Its bow ripped apart, fragments of it flying all over, some within only a few feet of the boys.

When the sound of the explosion died away, Bobby paused and looked back. Deep anguish overwhelmed him as he saw only a cloud of dark gray smoke rising slowly upward from the spot where the boat had sunk to its watery grave.

The boat had been a pride of his father's. Roger Canfield had left it at home only because Bobby had liked it so much, too.

Suddenly it occurred to him how close he must have been to death, and he shuddered. He thought of Walter, and fear gripped him as he wondered if Walter had been struck by the flying pieces of the boat.

He looked around anxiously, and relief came over him as he saw Walter about ten feet away, looking back at the grim pall of smoke and the floating debris.

"You all right?" Bobby asked.

"Yeah. How about you?" replied Walter.

"I'm okay."

Walter glanced toward shore. "That's a long way to swim," he observed.

"Wait a minute," said Bobby. "There should be some life jackets floating around."

They both looked around for the life jackets.

"There's one!" Walter shouted suddenly. "And there's another!"

Bobby saw the two life jackets that Walter was pointing to. Brushing aside the thought of the lost boat, he started to swim to one of them, while Walter swam to the other. They put the life jackets over their heads, buckled them, and tightened up the belts in front.

Seconds later a new sound reached Bobby's ears. It grew louder and louder. Looking about him, he saw a power boat speeding toward them. Two others were heading toward them from other directions.

"Looks like we won't have to swim it!" exclaimed Walter, smiling with relief.

"Right!" replied Bobby, feeling light and buoyant as the life jacket kept him afloat.

The nearest boat slowed down as it approached. There were two people in it, a man and a woman.

"Oh, wow!" yelled the woman, who looked to be in her early twenties. "I can't believe it! They're alive!"

Her eyes were wide as she stared at the two boys. Both she and the man were wearing swimsuits.

"Pull up beside him first," said the man, pointing toward Walter.

The woman, handling the steering wheel, drew up beside Walter, and the man proceeded to haul the boy into the boat. Then he hauled in Bobby.

"Anybody else besides you two in that boat?" the man inquired.

"No. It was just us," puffed Bobby, the water dripping off him.

"We heard the explosion and saw the fire. How could a boat explode? You boys were real lucky."

"I know," said Bobby, glancing at Walter. Would Walter tell, he wondered, what caused the explosion?

But Walter remained silent. He was sitting on one of the seats, his hair matted to his head, his clothes stuck to his skin, his attention drawn to the shore toward which they were heading.

"What happened?" the woman asked.

There was the inevitable question. And again Bobby waited for Walter to say something. But he didn't. He was ignoring them completely.

"I don't know," said Bobby. "The engine blew. We jumped out of the boat, then the gas tank blew."

I can't squeal on Walter, thought Bobby. *It's up to him to tell them how careless he's been.*

The man and woman exchanged a look.

"Where do you boys live?" the man asked.

"I live near the lake. Over there," said Bobby, pointing to the beach house that was easily visible.

"And you?" the man asked Walter.

"I live on Maple Avenue," said Walter.

The girl turned the wheel and headed the boat toward the beach house.

The man looked over Bobby's arms, legs, and body for bruises.

"I'm okay," Bobby assured him.

"I just want to check," replied the man.

He gave Walter a close looking-over too, then said, "I guess you're both all right." He sat back and relaxed, relieved that the boys weren't injured.

When they arrived on shore Bobby's mother was there waiting for them.

Thirteen

I JUST KNEW it was our boat!" cried Bobby's mother, hugging Bobby fiercely. "When I heard that explosion and then saw the boat was gone from the hoist — I just knew it!"

Bobby and Walter had removed their life jackets and had left them on the deck. The rescuers were leaving.

"You could have been killed!" his mother went on. "You know that? You could have been killed!"

Bobby didn't answer. He stood there, shivering, waiting for his mother to get hold of herself.

"What I would like to know," she said, staring directly at him, "is why you took the boat without permission. Explain *that* to me."

She was trembling, and her eyes were red from crying.

"I gave Walter a ride," Bobby answered. "I mean, that's why I—"

She looked at Walter, and frowned. "Walter? Walter who?"

"Walter Wilson."

"I don't think I've seen you before," she said, her voice softer now. "Where do you live, Walter?"

Walter looked at her. "On Maple Avenue," he answered calmly.

"Maple Avenue?" She stared at him. "That's about two miles from here. Do you play on Bobby's team? Is that why you're here?"

"No, ma'am."

"You just came to take a ride in the boat?"

"Yes, ma'am."

Bobby's mother glanced at Bobby, her

eyes probing. "I never heard you talk of him. Is he a new friend of yours?"

"No. He's . . ." Bobby couldn't get the words out.

"He's what?" his mother said, trying to wring the rest of the sentence out of him.

"You won't like to hear this, Mom," he said.

"I'm going to hear it sometime," she said. "You might as well tell it to me now."

He got up his gumption and formed the words in his mind first before uttering them. "He's the son of the woman Dad has been seeing lately," he said.

"Oh?" Her eyes widened, her cheeks flushed as she glanced back at Walter. "And because of that you felt that you should give him a ride in the boat? Is that it?"

"No, Mom. It wasn't like that at all. Walter told me that Dad had said it was okay." He paused, shivering, as he watched his mother staring at Walter Wilson. "I'm cold, Mom," he said. "I'd like to get out of these wet clothes."

She didn't answer him right away. She seemed too preoccupied with unpleasant thoughts.

"Come on," she said finally, drawing him toward the steps. "You, too, Walter. I'll drive you home."

"Crazy!" Roger Canfield shouted. "Crazy! Crazy! You're lucky you're alive, you know that? You and Walter both! Oh — wow!"

He had come over to the house as soon as he had heard from Walter about the boat's sinking. He had been at Walter's mother's house at the time, had heard Walter's version of the explosion and the sinking, and was here now to hear Bobby's.

He stood before Bobby, his chest heaving, his face wet with perspiration.

"One thing I want to get straight," he said firmly. "Walter told me that you were smoking a cigarette. That when you tossed it overboard, the wind blew it against the engine."

"He lied!" Bobby cried. "He's the one who

lighted a cigarette. He threw it away when I told him not to smoke.

"He told me he doesn't smoke," said Roger, looking deep into Bobby's eyes.

"The heck he doesn't! Dad, you know I don't smoke! I've never smoked a cigarette in my life!"

"That's true," said Bobby's mother. "If he had, I would have known about it."

Roger Canfield sighed. He was more composed now, his wits collected. "I believe you, Bobby. You've always been honest with your mother and me. Okay, that's all I want to know." He looked at his ex-wife. "There's a good insurance policy on that boat. You should get almost enough from it to buy another one, if you want to."

"I'll get the insurance money," she replied, gazing at him from behind amber sunglasses. "But I'll have to think about getting another boat. After what happened, I'm not sure I will. Anyway, I've already thought about it. I think it's only fair that you should have half of it."

"No. I don't need it," he said. "You can have all of it. That's not important to me."

"You sure?"

"I'm sure. I want to say, too, that it wasn't Bobby's fault that the boat blew up. I should have had that leaky line repaired a long time ago. I'm to blame for it." He paused. "Just the same, I've got a thing or two to say to that Walter." He turned to Bobby. "How come you gave him a ride in the boat in the first place?"

"Because he asked me to. He said that you told him it was all right for me to give him a ride."

Roger's mouth pursed. "I didn't tell him that at all. I guess I'll have to speak to him about that."

"Dad, I think that Walter is a pretty lonely kid who's looking for a friend or something," said Bobby. "Every time he says or does something, he's awkward about it. The more I'm near him, the more I've noticed it."

Roger frowned. "I've wondered about

that, Bobby," he said. He was quiet a moment or two, then he cleared his throat.
"Well, I'll go now. Unless something hap-
pens, I'll see you on Saturday morning.
Good-bye, Joyce."

"Good-bye, Roger."

He put on his yellow cap and walked out.
Bobby walked out with him. "Dad," he
said, thoughtfully, "whatever happened to
Walter's father?"

"He got killed a couple of years ago in
an automobile accident. Why?"

Bobby shrugged. "Just wondered."

Not until his father had entered his car
and driven off did Bobby go back into the
house and close the door.

He wasn't ripe for the game against the
Swallows. He didn't feel like playing baseball any more than he felt like flying to the
moon. And it wasn't the bruises that made
him feel like that. What few there were
wouldn't slow him up a bit.

It was the loss of the boat, and the almost

certain fact that his mother would not purchase another one to take its place.

Somehow, even though he hadn't used it much, the boat had been the one tangible thread that kept him close to his father during the weekdays. The weekends took care of themselves. The two were together then.

Nevertheless, he went to the game. He felt he had an obligation. Billy Trollop's father picked him up as usual in his big sedan.

The Sunbirds were up first and Bobby stepped to the plate, the bat feeling as if it weighed a ton. Red Burke, a tall right-hander with red, bushy eyebrows, was pitching for the Swallows. He had trouble finding the plate with his first three throws, and just like that the count was three and nothing.

Bobby stood at the plate, leaving the bat on his shoulder.

Red came back and placed his next two pitches directly over the heart of the plate, and then it was three and two.

Bobby stepped out of the box and killed a little time by rubbing his sweaty palms against his pants, and then rubbing the thin handle of his bat between his legs. The act wasn't only to dry the palms and the handle of the bat. It also provided a few seconds for some strong concentration.

But the few seconds didn't help Bobby. Red Burke breezed the next one in, just cutting the inside corner, and Bobby swung and missed.

He went back to the bench, embarrassed. It was the first time he had struck out while leading off.

"You can't steal bases if you don't get on, Fox," said Sherm, smiling at him.

"Glad you told me that," said Bobby.

Hank Spencer got the only hit during that half inning, a single through short.

B. J. Hendricks threw enough pitches to get out six men before he was able to vanquish the necessary three. And without allowing a run, at that.

In the top of the second inning Snoop

Myers, the utility infielder, singled after Billy Trollop had flied out, and Jake Shakespeare walked. Then Sherm was given a free ticket, too, loading the bases.

"Let's send up a designated hitter," said Eddie.

"Yeah, why don't we?" replied Hank enthusiastically.

"Because we don't have one, for one thing," said Bobby, who had gotten over most of his strikeout pain. "For another thing, it ain't in the rules."

Red Burke rifled in two strike pitches, and was about to go for his possible third, when B. J. stepped out of the box. The ump called time.

"Three men on, B. J.!" yelled Eddie. "Knock 'em in!"

B. J. stepped back into the box, bold, courageous, eager, and slammed a hot grounder to short. It was one of the quickest double plays in the league's history. Three outs.

The Swallows came up and began where

they had left off, banging out three hits in a row, including a long triple by their long-ball hitter, Tom Bootree. Two runs crossed the plate.

Top of the third. Bobby led off again, fouling the first two pitches, then forcing Red to throw four more before getting his well-earned walk.

On first base he looked for a sign from the third-base coach. *Play it safe.* He did, while Eddie took a strike call.

Then he got the sign he had somehow expected, even with the Sunbirds trailing by two runs. *Steal.*

He beat the throw by a mile.

"Thataway, Fox!" yelled a fan as Bobby stood on the bag, his hands on his hips.

Eddie flied out to right on the next pitch. Bobby, tagging up, had no trouble making it to third.

Hank reached out after an outside pitch and laid it over first base, bringing in Bobby. Then Andy tripled, scoring Hank. But that

was it as Billy and Snoop got out on a pop-up and a grounder, respectively.

"Your father must have been pretty sore when he heard about the boat," said Billy, as he sat next to Bobby on the bench.

"Don't think he wasn't," said Bobby. "On top of the accident, Walter told him that *I* was the cause of the fire. That *I* lit the cigarette."

"Wow. Your father didn't believe that bull, did he?"

"Not really. That was why he came over to talk with me about it. Anyway, I don't think it's all Walter's fault, and I told my father that."

Billy looked at him. "What do you mean?"

"Do you know that Walter's father is dead? That he was killed in an accident?"

"No."

"Well, he was," said Bobby. "I think that has a lot to do with the way Walter behaves. He tries to pretend he's cool, except that he makes a fool of himself and doesn't know it."

Suddenly the thought occurred to him: *Have I been acting that way, too? Oh, man!*

The Swallows picked up one run during their turn at bat. But the Sunbirds came through for two more in the top of the fourth, during which Bobby chalked up his second stolen base of the game after belting out a liner over the second-base bag.

Horse collars went up on the scoreboard until the bottom of the fifth when the Swallows drove in two runs, then held the Sunbirds scoreless the last two innings.

It was 5–4, in the Swallows' favor, when the game ended.

Fourteen

*R*OGER CANFIELD arrived at ten minutes of nine Saturday morning, picked up Bobby, and drove to Meadow Park.

"I see that they're calling you the Fox," he said as they drove slowly and quietly through the streets of Lyncook. "That's quite a tag."

"You wouldn't believe who stuck it on me," exclaimed Bobby.

"Oh, yes, I would," replied his father, chuckling. "I was there when those two kids watching you practice base stealing called you Fox. Remember?"

"Oh, that's right," said Bobby, now recalling the day vividly. "I remember." He laughed. "I can think of worse names than that!"

"Right. The only thing about Fox is, you'll have to keep working hard to live up to it. And I think you will. You're doing fine."

Bobby looked at his father. "Were you at the game Thursday, Dad?"

"No. I'm not always free in the afternoons. I read about you in last night's paper. There wasn't much, but it's usually the winning team that gets most of the publicity, anyway."

Not always free in the afternoons? Where was he? Visiting Mrs. Wilson?

No sooner had the thought popped into Bobby's mind than he felt ashamed of himself. He shouldn't have thought that of his father. What his father did was his business. Anyway, what was so bad about his visiting Mrs. Wilson? He was divorced. And she was a widow.

153

Darn! he thought. *What am I doing? Getting on my father because I love him so? Should I close my eyes to all the things he does, and open them only when I'm with him? Doing things with him? What is the right thing to do?*

He didn't know. But deep in his heart he wished that his father would not see another woman. Not ever.

They reached the park. Roger Canfield parked the car and locked it, taking no chance even though the car was six years old.

They got out and walked toward the picnic pavilion, beyond which was the sandy beach. For a while they talked about baseball, and Bobby's growing experience as a hitter and a base stealer. Being both was extraordinary, according to his father, for all good hitters were not base stealers. Dave Kingman, Mike Schmidt, Greg Luzinski, a few of the names that rolled off his tongue, were good with the stick, but once on base — unless they drove the ball out

154

of the park — they usually left it up to the next batters to move them along.

Base stealing was an extra talent inherent in one whose body had a natural development for speed and coordination. It wasn't everyone who was blessed with those physical attributes. Bobby had them. All he had to do was to keep working on them, and not to let them get dormant. Roger Canfield talked as if he enjoyed saying what he was saying. He knew baseball from top to bottom and sideways, having played in the minors for five years after graduating from high school.

Somehow Bobby had the feeling that his father was sorry he had quit at so early an age, but his father had never said so.

They found an empty bench on the beach and sat down. Neither said a word for several minutes. They just watched the waves lapping up on shore, people swimming, and sailboats leaning against the wind.

Then his father said something that gave

Bobby a start. Not sure he had heard right, Bobby looked closely at his father. "What did you say, Dad?"

"I said that I'm taking a job on a freighter," repeated Roger Canfield. "I've always wanted to take a trip around the world. This time I'm going to do it."

Bobby stared at him. The thought that he wouldn't see his father for many months frightened him to the bone. "You're going to quit your job?"

"I'll have to."

For a long minute Bobby was silent. "How — how long will you be gone, Dad?" he asked finally.

"Could be a year. It depends. If I like it, I might stay with it."

Bobby felt an ache in his throat. He hated to ask the next question, but he had to. "You going to take anybody with you, Dad?"

"No. I'm going alone."

That meant he wouldn't be taking Mrs. Wilson. He had no intention of marrying her, then. That thought made Bobby feel slightly better, anyway.

"Can I go with you?"

The question was crazy to ask. He knew that, but there was always that one-in-a-million chance that the answer would be "yes."

"You know you can't, Bobby," said his father, pricking his son's dream balloon. "It's just impossible. No, I'm going alone. I'll miss you very much, but I've got to get away from here for a while. It's — it's hard to explain."

"That's okay, Dad. You don't have to explain."

Restless, that was the word in a nutshell. His mother had mentioned it dozens of times. Roger Canfield was the most restless man on earth. He couldn't stay put in one place for any length of time. He couldn't hold onto a job for any length of time. There was something in his blood, she said, that egged him on to other places, to do other things. That she had lived with him as long as she had was a miracle.

"I got the truth out of Walter about that smoking business," his father said, changing the subject. "He admitted he had lied."

Bobby met his father's eyes. "I bet he had a tough time admitting it."

"Yes, he did."

"You won't ever marry Mrs. Wilson, will you, Dad?" said Bobby earnestly.

His father's eyes shone. "No. And that's a promise. As a matter of fact, I've stopped seeing her." He paused. "Talking about the Wilsons, when is your team going to play Walter's again? I don't want to miss it."

"I'm not sure. Maybe next week."

"Okay. I'll keep my eye on the papers."

At Municipal Park that afternoon they watched the Lyncook Giants beat the Valley Bobcats. The next day Roger Canfield borrowed a 12-foot boat from a friend of his, and, using fishpoles that he still kept in the beach house, spent the whole day fishing with his son. It was, Bobby thought, like having a good-bye supper with his father.

He had a so-so day against the Redlegs on Tuesday, getting one walk and no hits. But he had one stolen base, and the Sunbirds had taken the game, 8–6.

It was on Thursday that they played the Cowbirds. A big crowd attended. Among them were the two long-haired fans whose names Bobby still did not know.

"Hi ya, Fox. How you doin'?" one of them asked, grinning.

"Okay," he said. "How about you?"

"Just great," came the response.

His father was among the first to come, as if to make sure of his seat near the third-base sack. He smiled and waved, saying a lot just in those silent gestures.

His father's words rang again in Bobby's ears, tolling in the back of his mind. *I've always wanted to take a trip around the world. This time I'm going to do it.* He tried to concentrate on the game. How

159

could he play a good game of baseball if he kept thinking all the time of his father and what his father was going to do?

Grandpa Alex was there, too, wearing a hat to cover his bald head, and dark glasses to shield his eyes from the glaring sun.

The sight of them warmed Bobby's heart. Next to his father, Grandpa Alex was the greatest living man on earth.

The Sunbirds had first bats.

"Look who's on the mound," Billy said as Bobby started swinging two bats, each with a metal doughnut around the fat part.

"I see," observed Bobby, who hadn't thought much about it. He had other — more important — thoughts on his mind.

"Play ball!" the umpire announced.

The crowd cheered and clapped.

"Get a hit, Bobby! Get on, kid!" a fan yelled.

"Come on, Fox! Start it off!" another fan chimed in.

Bobby tossed aside one of the bats, removed the doughnut from the one he kept, and stepped to the plate. He dug into the dirt for secure footing, then held up his bat and looked across the short span between home and the mound at Walter Wilson.

Walter looked big, strong, and menacing. He looked as if he could throw a ball two hundred miles an hour, and was going to do it with every pitch.

He stepped on the rubber, stretched, and delivered. The ball streaked in, knee-high and a hair inside. Bobby heard it explode in the catcher's mitt.

"Strike!" boomed the ump.

Bobby looked back at him in surprise. The ump, busy adjusting his counter, ignored him.

Another pitch.

"Strike two!"

Bobby stepped out of the box. He wasn't happy about that call, either.

"Come on, Fox!" yelled one of the long-haired fans. "You can't steal a base if you don't get on!"

He stepped back into the box. Then

161

Walter proceeded to fire four more pitches, all balls.

Bobby walked.

He looked for the sign from the third-base coach. *Play it safe.*

Eddie took a called strike.

Then it came — thumb to cap, to belt, to chest, and back to cap. The steal was on.

Fifteen

*B*OBBY LOOKED up at the crowd and saw his father and grandfather. Both were watching him intently, waiting to see if he would run. Grandpa Alex then leaned over and said something to Bobby's father.

Bobby reverted his attention to Walter, who was getting set to pitch.

I wonder if seeing me will make him think about that boat accident, thought Bobby. *I wonder if he feels sorry at all that he had lied to my father.*

Bobby took his lead.

I've got to make this one good, he promised himself, forgetting Walter and his connection with the boat accident for a minute. *I've got to show Dad that all that training paid off.*

Walter stretched, brought down his arms. Then, like a shot, he fired the ball to first.

The throw could not have been more accurate, nor quicker. The first baseman caught the ball near the bag and tagged Bobby on the leg just a fraction of a second before he could get back.

"Ouuuut!" shouted the ump.

Bobby trotted to the Sunbirds' bench, his head bowed in embarrassment, as hooplas exploded from the Cowbirds' fans.

Sympathetic remarks came from the two long-haired kids. "That's okay, Fox. Don't let it get you down. You'll be up again."

They were okay guys. At a time like this he could use all the moral support he could get.

But he had let his father and grandfather down. That's what bothered him.

164

Eddie smashed a single to left, only to perish on first as both Hank and Andy failed to connect with safeties.

B. J., pitching for the Sunbirds, gave up a hit and a walk as the Cowbirds came to bat. But that was all.

Billy, leading off in the top of the second, connected with a high fly that might have landed in the middle of the lake, if it had traveled horizontally. As it was, Nick Tully, the Cowbirds' shortstop, caught it just outside of the base path.

Walter rifled in two pitches to Snoop Myers. Both were balls.

Then he accidentally laid one in where Snoop must have seen it hanging like a balloon. Swinging with all his might, Snoop met the ball right at its equator and sent it out of the park.

Cheers exploded from the fans as Snoop circled the bases. Even the Cowbirds' fans gave him an ovation. Snoop took off his cap and politely bowed.

The next two batters, Toody and Sherm, went down without a hit.

Again the Cowbirds, and again the Sunbirds, breezed through their turns at bat without scoring a run. Walter had made a threat by driving out a long double, but good defense on the part of Eddie and Snoop had kept him from going any farther than second base.

The big blast happened in the bottom of the third. It started with B. J. walking Jake Hollister, who went to third on a sharp two-bagger by Larry Jones. Then Adam Hooton singled, scoring Jake.

Bobby called time and trotted to the mound, thinking that B. J. needed a few minutes' rest to get himself back in order. Andy, Eddie, and Snoop joined the huddle.

"Take it easy, B. J.," said Bobby. "You're working too fast."

"Keep 'em low," suggested Andy.

"Just get 'em out," offered Snoop.

The three infielders returned to their posi-

166

tions, leaving B. J. alone with his problem. Nick Tully swung at B. J.'s first pitch, a long fly ball to left field. Hank put it away with ease.

"Thataway to go, old fella!" exclaimed Bobby.

Up came Foster Moore, the Cowbirds' burly center fielder, waving his bat over his head like a war club. Everybody backed up, knowing Foster's power.

Bang! He sliced a single over short, and Larry scored.

Walter came up again, keeping the Sunbirds playing deep. Batting seventh meant that he was one of those rare birds, a hitting pitcher.

He proved it again on the third pitch. The blow looked as if it might be a home run as the ball soared to deep center field. But it struck the fence and bounced back, and Walter finished up on third. A run had scored on the hit, and the Cowbirds went out in front, 4–1.

I don't know why I should feel sorry for him, thought Bobby. *He hits like a fool on the ball field.*

Second baseman Ed Michaels kept up the hitting barrage with a run-driving-in single, and Bobby began to wonder just how long this merry-go-round would last. There was still only one out, and the Cowbirds were hitting the old apple as if they couldn't get out if they tried.

Butch Mortz, the last man on the totem pole for the Cowbirds, then slashed a hot grounder to Bobby. Bobby caught it on a hop, fired the ball to second, and Eddie relayed it to first. A double play!

"Oh, wow," murmured Bobby under his breath as he trotted off the field. "It's about time."

"Maybe you ought to take me out, Coach," said B. J., slump-shouldered as he sat back against the dugout wall. "They're making mincemeat out of me."

Coach Tarbell looked at him. "I want you to pitch this game, B. J. Ollie's only had one day's rest. Take your time out there. Don't rush it, and you'll come through A-okay. All right?"

B. J. shrugged. "You're the boss, Coach," he said.

Leading off, Snoop Myers again surprised everyone by banging out a safe hit, even though it was only a single. Toody walked, and Sherm socked the first pitch for a streaking double between left and center fields. Snoop and Toody scored.

B. J., whom no one expected to hit safely, didn't. However, he managed to get on, thanks to an error by Nick Tully, the Cowbirds' shortstop.

With runners on first and second, Bobby was up again. He thought of his father and grandfather sitting in the stands, watching him, waiting to see what he would do. He remembered what had happened to him during that first inning when he had tried to steal. He had certainly flubbed badly then.

What was he going to show them now?

He looked at Walter, and waited for the pitch he wanted. He got it after three pitches, an over-the-heart-of-the-plate fastball.

But the blow was just a solid smash down to short, and Nick threw him out.

Well, at least he had hit the ball. That was a consolation.

Eddie came through with a single, driving in Sherm. The run brought the Sunbirds up to within one score of the Cowbirds, 5–4. The Sunbirds were back in the ball game.

Then Hank hit into a double play, and the top of the fourth inning was over.

Only Larry Jones managed to get on base as the Cowbirds took their turns at the plate. He died on first, however.

In the top of the fifth, Billy got a single and advanced to second on Nick's ground-ball error, a grass-streaker hit by Toody. But they perished on the bases, too.

B. J. mowed down Ed Michaels with a strikeout, then got support from Billy as the center fielder hauled in Butch Mortz's cloud-scraping fly. Jake Hollister made the third out.

"Okay, B. J.," said Snoop as the left-hander headed for the plate. "Start it off. I guarantee something's going to happen."

B. J. obliged by dropping a single over first. Then Bobby, his fourth time at bat, came up with his first hit. *It's about time,* he thought.

He didn't look for his father and grand-father now. He didn't have to. Part of that applause he heard must be theirs.

But suddenly, he remembered that his father would be gone soon. And an ache lodged in his throat.

Change your mind, Dad, he pleaded. *Please change your mind.*

Neither Eddie nor Hank was able to hit balls where they weren't. But Andy came through with a smashing drive over short, scoring B. J. to tie up the ball game, 5–5.

The Sunbirds' bench went wild. The fans

went crazy. You would have thought it was Shea Stadium with the Mets coming from behind to tie it up with the Phillies.

Billy kept the game rolling with a walk. Then Snoop smashed one through the shortstop's legs, scoring Bobby and putting the Sunbirds ahead, 6–5. Toody grounded out.

"We're in! We're in!" Snoop shouted wildly as he came running in for his glove.

"The ball game isn't over yet," reminded Walter, heading for his bench.

He was right. In the Cowbirds' half of the inning a single by Ted Lacey, then a triple off the big bat of Jake Hollister knotted the score again, 6–6.

The moments got hairier when the Sunbirds came up as Bobby, third man in the batting order, watched Sherm go to the plate and fly out. Next up was B. J., who made it two outs by grounding out to first.

"Take the last one, Walt!" shouted Butch Mortz, the Cowbirds' catcher, as Bobby stepped into the batting box.

Bobby ignored him. He dug his toes into the dirt and waited for Walter to come to him.

Walter did, on the second pitch. Bobby drove it over second base, a clean single.

He couldn't believe it. He needed that hit. The team needed it.

He glanced over to the third-base coaching box. The steal sign was on!

He took his lead, careful this time not to go too far. Walter got set, then snapped the ball to first.

Bobby scooted back in time.

Keep throwing them over here, Walter, he wanted to say. One bad throw and I'm gone.

As it was, he didn't have to wait for a bad throw. He went down on the pitch, and made it by a mile.

He could hear his father's and grandfather's cheers. And he looked at the crowd and saw them standing up together, clapping like crazy. His heart tingled.

Again he sized up the situation. There was no steal sign being offered him by the third-base coach. But would that master-mind on the mound, Walter Wilson, expect him to steal third with two outs?

Walter got set to pitch, and Bobby got set to run. On the pitch, Bobby took off. Eddie's swing and miss helped, for the catcher failed to get the ball to third on time, and Bobby was safe.

"Hey, Fox!" yelled one of his long-haired fans enthusiastically. "You made it, man!"

"Steal home, Fox!" shouted the other half of the pair.

Steal home? No way!

But — why not? *Why not?* Who would expect him to steal home with two outs? Maybe those two long-haired fans of his. But who else?

The more he considered the idea, the better it sounded.

He sized up the situation. There was a fifty-fifty chance of Eddie's getting a safe hit.

Maybe less. His failure to hit would mean that the Cowbirds, taking their last bats, would have three outs to make in their attempt to break the tie.

I'll have to try it, decided Bobby. *It makes sense.* Thanks, kid! he wanted to yell to the long-haired fan who had suggested the idea.

He took a lead, standing straight so that Walter would not get any silly thoughts about him. That he catch Walter — and Butch — off guard was of utmost importance.

Walter stretched, glanced briefly at Bobby, then started his delivery. At the same time, Bobby started to dash for home.

Running as fast as he could go, he was within a few yards of home when he saw the ball strike Butch's mitt. There was only one thing he could do now, and he did it. He hit the dirt. Sliding across the plate, he saw Butch falling over it toward him.

Butch put the ball on him. But the call that boomed from the umpire told the story.

"Safe!"

"Thataboy, Fox!" yelled his long-haired fans. "You did it, man! You did it!"

From the stands came the booming cheers of the other Sunbirds fans. Bobby's father and grandfather joined in the cheering. It was the happiest moment of his life.

The half inning ended as Eddie flied out.

Adam led off at the bottom of the seventh with a single. Nick flied out, then Foster hit into a double play, and it was over; 7–6, in favor of the Sunbirds.

Bobby's father and grandfather came off the stands. But they had to wait for the mob that surrounded their hero to disperse before they could get to him.

"So they call you the Fox, do they?" exclaimed Grandpa Alex, his eyes twinkling with admiration. "Well, you certainly deserve it. Guess all that practice that your father and I put you through helped, didn't it?"

"It sure did, Grandpa!" replied Bobby happily.

His father beamed with pride. "Man, you can *run*," he said. "And don't let anybody tell you different!"

Bobby smiled. "Thanks, Dad." He paused, his mind suddenly shifting to another, more personal, matter. "Dad, are you still going?"

"On that freighter job? Yes, Bobby, I am. But, don't worry. I'll be back. And who knows? Probably by then things might change. You can never tell."

"No, Dad," said Bobby. "I guess you can't."

Maybe it is best this way, thought Bobby.

It was a good feeling to know for certain that his father would be coming back, and, who knew, by that time he might just be the best base stealer in the state.

How many of these Matt Christopher sports classics have you read?

Baseball
- [ ] Catcher with a Glass Arm
- [ ] The Fox Steals Home
- [ ] The Kid Who Only Hit Homers
- [ ] Look Who's Playing First Base
- [ ] Miracle at the Plate
- [ ] No Arm in Left Field
- [ ] Shortstop from Tokyo
- [ ] Year Mom Won the Pennant

Basketball
- [ ] Johnny Long Legs

Dirt Bike Racing
- [ ] Dirt Bike Racer
- [ ] Dirt Bike Runaway

Football
- [ ] Catch That Pass!
- [ ] Football Fugitive
- [ ] Tight End
- [ ] Touchdown for Tommy
- [ ] Tough to Tackle

Ice Hockey
- [ ] Face-Off
- [ ] Ice Magic

Soccer
- [ ] Soccer Halfback

Track
- [ ] Run, Billy, Run

All available in paperback from
Little, Brown and Company